WASHINGTON

SOLEDUCK RIVER
HOH RIVER
QUEETS RIVER
QUINAULT RIVER

SKAGIT RIVER
WENATCHEE RIVER

OKANAGAN RIVER
COLUMBIA RIVER
PEND OREILLE RIVER
KOOTENAI RIVER
FLATHEAD RIVER

SPOKANE RIVER
COEUR D'ALENE
CLARK FORK

COWLITZ RIVER
LEWIS RIVER
COLUMBIA RIVER

KLICKITAT RIVER
YAKIMA RIVER

ST. JOE RIVER
BITTERROOT RIVER

SNAKE RIVER
CLEARWATER RIVER
GRANDE RONDE RIVER

MONTANA

COLUMBIA RIVER BASIN

WILLAMETTE RIVER
DESCHUTES RIVER
JOHN DAY RIVER

SALMON RIVER
SNAKE RIVER

WYO MING

SIUSLAW RIVER
UMPQUA RIVER
ROGUE RIVER

PAYETTE RIVER
BOISE RIVER

OREGON

IDAHO

CONTINENTAL DIVIDE

SMITH RIVER

KLAMATH RIVER

NEVADA

OWYHEE
BRUNEAU RIVER
SNAKE RIVER

BEAR RIVER

GREEN RIVER

PACIFIC COASTAL BASIN

MAD RIVER
EEL RIVER

SACRAMENTO RIVER
FEATHER RIVER
RUSSIAN RIVER

HUMBOLDT RIVER

WEBER RIVER
JORDAN RIVER
PROVO RIVER

YAMPA RIVER
WHITE RIVER

TRUCKEE RIVER
AMERICAN RIVER
MOKELUMNE RIVER
STANISLAUS RIVER
TUOLUMNE RIVER
MERCED RIVER

CARSON RIVER
WALKER RIVER

GREAT BASIN

WHITE RIVER

SEVIER RIVER

COLORADO RIVER

GUNNISON RIVER

COLO RADO

SAN JOAQUIN RIVER

KINGS RIVER
OWENS RIVER

UTAH

SAN JUAN RIVER

SALINAS RIVER
KERN RIVER

VIRGIN RIVER

COLORADO RIVER BASIN

LITTLE COLORADO

CALI FOR NIA

ARIZONA

COLORADO RIVER

NEW MEX ICO

GILA RIVER
SALT RIVER
GILA RIVER

Gulf of California

Rivers of the West

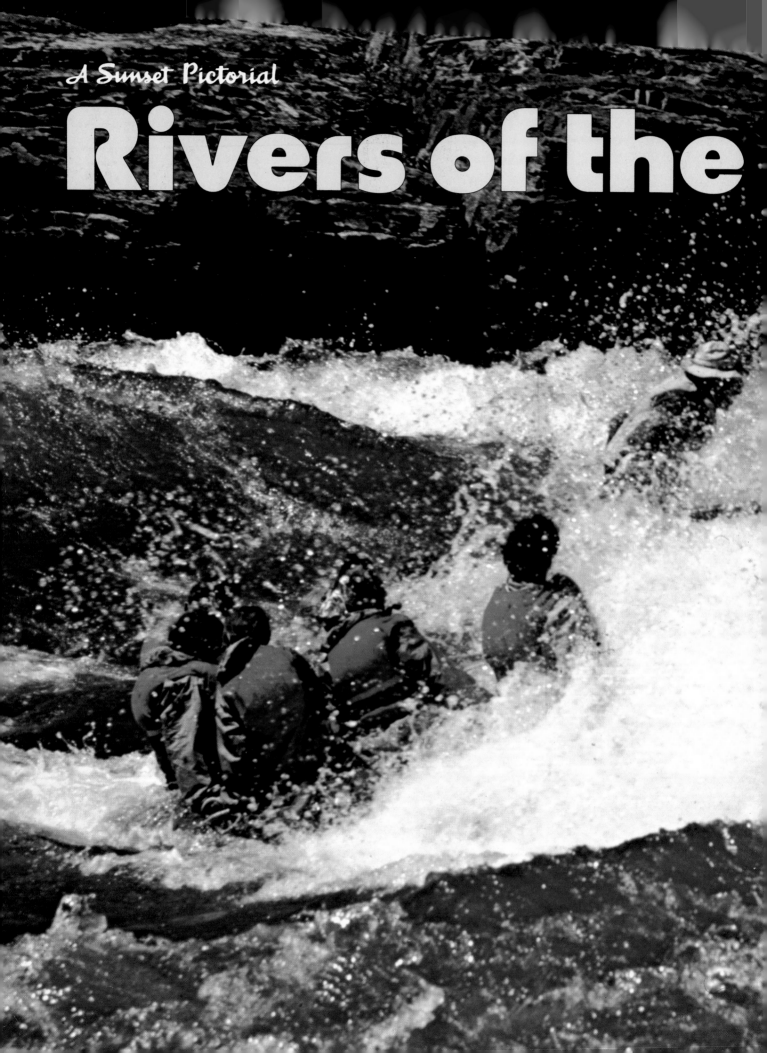

Rivers of the

West

Lane Publishing Co., Menlo Park, California

CONTENTS

Edited by Elizabeth Hogan

Design and Layout
Henry Rasmussen

Illustrations and Maps
Steven Jacobs Design

Executive Editor, Sunset Books
David E. Clark

Front cover: Salmon fishing on the Willamette River, near Oregon City, by Ted Streshinsky.
Back cover: Tuolumne River in Yosemite National Park, by Ted Streshinsky.
Title Page photo: Rafting the Snake River Canyon, by Ron Cohen.
Endsheet map: Rivers on Western side of Continental Divide, by Susan Colton.

First Printing October 1974

RIVERS OF THE WEST   6
A Resource - Vital but Vulnerable

COLUMBIA RIVER BASIN   14
The Most Water in the West

The Columbia River   16
Powerhouse of the West
The Spokane & Pend Oreille   40
In a Land of Lakes, Some Rivers, Too
The Yakima & Wenatchee   48
Heart of Apple Country
The Willamette River   56
Lifeline of Oregon
The Deschutes & John Day   74
Oregon's Lonely Rivers
The Snake River   84
Once the "Accursed Mad River"
More Rivers in the Columbia Basin   102

COLORADO RIVER BASIN   104
Precious Water for the Southwest

The Colorado River   106
Highly Respected, Greatly Overworked
The Green River   128
Shades of the Colorado
The Salt River   138
Keeping Phoenix Alive
More Rivers in the Colorado Basin   150

PACIFIC COASTAL BASIN 152
From the Mountains to the Sea

The Sacramento & San Joaquin 154
Main Arteries in the Central Valley
The Sierra Rivers 174
They Offer Something for Everyone
The Coastal Rivers 190
Colorfully Named . . . Little Used
More Rivers in the Coastal Basin 204

GREAT BASIN 206
Rivers Never Reach the Sea

The Humboldt River 208
Nevada's Big One
The Owens River 214
Little Known but Heavily Relied Upon
More Rivers in the Great Basin 220

SUGGESTED READINGS 222

INDEX 224

SPECIAL FEATURES

River Talk **13**
Life Cycle of the Salmon **27**
Log Moving **32**
Where Western Rivers Begin and End **82**
River Names — Rooted in History **92**
Experiencing a River **100**
The Colorado . . . Slave to Seven States **111**
When a River Created a Sea **127**
River Runners at their Daily Routine **134**
Paddle Wheelers on Western Waters **157**
Waterfowl . . . Home is Where the River is **166**
California's "Power-full" Rivers **180**
Reckless Rivers — Mostly Tamed **193**
Rivers that Give Los Angeles its Water **219**

MAPS

The Columbia River **17** • The Spokane &
Pend Oreille Rivers **41** • The Yakima &
Wenatchee Rivers **49** • The Willamette
River **56** • The Deschutes & John Day
Rivers **75** • The Snake River **85** • The
Colorado River **107** • The Green River **129**
The Salt River **139** • The Sacramento & San
Joaquin Rivers **155** • The Sierra Rivers **174**
The Coastal Rivers **191** • The Humboldt
River **209** • The Owens River **214**

RIVERS OF
A Resource - Vital

THE WEST but Vulnerable

A river is more than an amenity. It is a treasure. Oliver Wendell Holmes.

Man has often succeeded in establishing cities and factories in wilderness areas. But in the delicate balance between civilization and wilderness, wilderness has, more often than not, suffered. So it has been with the rivers of the West. Settlers and entrepreneurs and vacationists in the past have often put rivers to work, little heeding the consequences to the nature of the rivers. Only within the last decade have we become concerned about preserving the natural beauty of our resources—one of the most important of which is our rivers.

How do rivers serve our needs? In the West our rivers supply us with drinking water, energy for our homes and industries, and water to grow food. They serve as highways for transporting goods. They are home to fish and aquatic plants and animals. And Western rivers offer some of the finest water recreation found anywhere.

In order for us to use the rivers as sources of power and water, we have controlled every major Western waterway with dams, dramatically altering their character. Sometimes we have abused them, destroying the quality of their water with industrial and municipal waste.

But all is not lost with the rivers in the West. Federal and state agencies and environmental groups are working to keep the remaining rivers or sections of tampered-with rivers free-flowing. The badly polluted Western rivers have been cleaned up or are undergoing cleanup campaigns. Although what has been lost cannot be regained, what is still here can be saved.

Which Rivers are Western and Why?

A great divide of mountains running north and south across the western half of the North American continent determines whether rivers will head toward the Atlantic Ocean or the Pacific Ocean. Water running down the eastern slope flows toward the Atlantic; water rushing down the western side journeys toward the Pacific Ocean. *Rivers of the West* deals with rivers on the Western side of the Continental Divide.

Western rivers fall into four separate basins, or drainage areas. They are the Columbia River Basin (in the Pacific Northwest), the Colorado River Basin (in the Southwest), the Pacific Coastal Basin (along the Pacific Coast), and the Great Basin (between the Sierra Nevada and Wasatch Range). Each of the four chapters in the book is devoted to one of these basins.

Rivers in the Columbia River Basin all feed into the Columbia River, either directly or through a system of tributaries. Rivers in the Colorado River Basin eventually meet the Colorado River. Waterways in the Pacific Coastal Basin and the Great Basin do not center around any single river. Instead, they are groupings of individual rivers that have common endings. Those in the Coastal Basin drain directly into the Pacific Ocean; those in the Great Basin are landlocked, ending in dry or still active lakes.

(For a map of Western rivers and their basins, turn to either the inside front or back cover.)

The Role of Rivers in History

Throughout the ages, rivers and civilizations have gone side by side. The annual flooding of the Nile River turned desert lands into agricultural fields, supporting one of the oldest and greatest civilizations of all. Along the Tigris and Euphrates rivers thrived the Sumerian and Babylonian civilizations.

In the New World, rivers were first the routes of explorations, later highways for commerce. In the Western United States, prehistoric Indians made their homes near water. Spaniards crossed and followed many a river in exploring the uncharted territory north of Mexico. Fur-trappers relied on the rivers for their living. Pathfinders and settlers followed river routes west.

Although many people passed along the

Inundated by The Dalles. At Celilo Falls, local Indians fished for salmon with pulleys and dip nets. Since 1957 this breathtaking sight and the fishing grounds have lain at the bottom of the reservoir behind The Dalles Dam. If you drive the route of the Columbia River today, you'll find it hard to imagine that this wide, placid river once sported such a dramatic natural falls.

A distinctive difference! In the Columbia River Basin, rivers generally flow through mountains and forests. Those in the Colorado River Basin travel the desert areas, funneling through steep canyons and rocky plateaus. At left is Oregon's McKenzie River, a tributary to the Willamette and part of the Columbia's system. Below is the Colorado River swinging through the Grand Canyon.

RON COHEN

rivers, surprisingly few settlements were established along river banks. Several cities, such as Oregon City on the Willamette River, Sacramento on the Sacramento River, and Spokane on the Spokane River did emerge as part of the Western movement.

The Eternal Life of a River

Natural, free-flowing bodies of water, rivers are part of an eternal water cycle. Heat from the sun lifts water from the seas in the form of water vapor. Water evaporates from lakes and rivers. Plants and animals also give off water vapor. All this moisture condenses, forming clouds that are carried over the land. Water returns to the earth as rain or snow and once again is drawn by gravity toward the sea. Some of the water may seep through the soil to be stored temporarily as ground water, surfacing as springs or running out into stream channels.

Rivers--Older than the Hills

No matter what direction rivers run, they always travel downhill. Beginning miles from where they will end, rivers pursue paths mapped out over the ages by the erosive action of the water and the internal forces of the earth.

Geologists sometimes refer to rivers as "young," "middle-aged," or "old." These terms describe the condition of the landscape carved by the river, not the actual age of the river—for rivers sometimes date back billions of years. In its "youth", a river plunges rapidly downhill, cutting through narrow valleys. As a river matures, it meanders gently through broad valleys, bounded by smoothly rounded hills. In old age, a river curves widely across nearly flat plains, with the surrounding hills almost completely worn away.

The Changed Character of our Western Rivers

The personalities of today's Western rivers differ sharply from what they were during explorer days. The main change has been damming. Every major Western river has been dammed. At the bottom of the flatwater reservoir created by a dam lies the true character of a river—its current, its soul.

But damming has enabled the West to grow. About 80 per cent of the Pacific

Introduction 9

Northwest's energy comes from hydroelectric power. Power generated at Hoover Dam serves three states. Energy generated on California rivers provide Californians with a healthy percentage of their power. Such water projects as the Columbia Basin Project, the Salt River Project, and the Central Valley Project have irrigated thousands of acres of formerly unproductive lands. Flood control dams have enabled unpredictable flows to be used year-round and have saved lives and dollars taming rampages.

In addition to damming, man has had an effect on the quality of river water. Population centers sitting along rivers have sometimes used the river for a dumping ground, creating an overdose of bacteria that leads to a depletion of oxygen in the water—and hence pollution.

Western Rivers -- Cleaner Today than Yesterday?

Fortunately, Western rivers do not suffer the heavy pollution problems that plague their Eastern counterparts. The reason is simple. Most Western rivers are not straddled so extensively with industrial and metropolitan areas—they have not been the recipient of industrial waste or raw sewage to anywhere near the same degree as Eastern waterways.

One Western river—the Willamette—did suffer heavily from an indiscriminate dumping of waste. But within the last decade, the river has been cleaned up and flows about 90 per cent cleaner.

Not polluted to the degree that the Willamette was, the Spokane River received a cleaning and a facelift in conjunction with the 1974 World's Fair. Utah's Jordan River is also undergoing a cleanup campaign.

A problem of a different nature—but still a problem—is the salinity carried in the lower Colorado River. Where improper logging or road construction has taken place, sediment can cause survival problems for insects and fish in stream bottoms. A high discharge of nutrients into waterways can cause an abnormal growth of algae.

Hopefully the problems that have faced rivers in the past can be avoided in the future if private and public agencies become aware of the effects they may be having on waterways. A big help to all rivers is the 1972 Federal Water Pollution Control Act, requiring each state to develop a comprehensive plan for alleviating any problems in its waters.

A river running free. Near its headwaters, a river churns wildly, showing its most glorious side. But as a river pursues its path, it usually runs into controls imposed by man. This holds true with the Kings River. In Kings Canyon National Park, it flows freely, but below the park, the river is blocked and stored for massive irrigation use in California's Central Valley.

Preserving our Free-Flowing Streams

Although many Western rivers have been tamed, some—such as the Middle Fork of the Salmon, the Middle Fork of the Feather, the St. Joe, the Coeur d'Alene, and the Smith—have escaped the hand of man. The future looks bright for these and other rivers, for environmental groups and public agencies are working hard to preserve the natural state of our waterways and their surrounding lands.

In 1968 the Federal Government enacted a Wild and Scenic Rivers Act to make sure that certain rivers or sections of rivers remain in their free-flowing conditions. To be included in the program, a river had to be substantially free flowing, of high water quality, or in a position to be restored to high quality. The river and the adjacent lands had to be in a natural or esthetically pleasing condition, be hospitable to fish and wildlife, and possess outstanding scenic, recreational, geological, historical, and cultural values.

Eight rivers were included in the initial act, four of which are in the West. They are the Middle Fork of the Feather, the Middle Fork of the Clearwater, the Middle Fork of the Salmon, and the Rogue. Twenty-seven other rivers are under study for classification in the system; among them are eight Western rivers—the Bruneau, Illinois, Flathead, Moyie, Priest, Salmon, St. Joe, and Skagit.

In addition, some states are establishing their own programs for protecting the natural character of certain rivers. Oregon's scenic waterways program includes a segment of the Rogue, the Illinois, the Deschutes, the Minam, the Owyhee, and the John Day. Colorado's study included the Gunnison, the Green, and the South Fork of the Dolores. New Mexico's program will include the Upper Gila. California's system involves portions of the Klamath, Trinity, Smith, Eel, and American river systems.

A New American Experience

Canoeists, fishermen, swimmers, and hikers have always enjoyed Western rivers. But now white-water boating enthusiasts are flocking to certain Western waterways during spring, summer, and fall to "run the rapids." Commercial float trips—especially those that last only a weekend—fill up almost as soon as schedules come out. River running attracts

A river at work. Man has put Western rivers to work producing energy, irrigating fields, and supplying people with water. The main reason for damming the Spokane River in Spokane, Washington, was for hydroelectric power.

not only Westerners but also Easterners. People from Illinois, New Jersey, and Maryland thrill to the excitement of the West's wild water.

Perhaps the overwhelming popularity of river running is related to our desire to return to nature—to get away from the increasing pressures of everyday life. A river trip can take you totally away from civilization—away from newspapers, radios, cars. The only sounds you hear are the roaring waters, oars dipping through calm water, and the songs of native birds.

Whenever you are on the water—swimming, rafting, fishing—the nature of the river must be kept in mind. A river's current is a powerful force, and that force must be respected.

A Look into the Future

Although several river control projects are underway (the Central Arizona Project taking the Colorado River to central Arizona; the new Auburn Dam on the American River), future damming and channeling of river water will probably come under question. Is damming (whether for hydroelectric power, irrigation, flood control, water supply) the only and the best solution? The 9-mile stretch of white water on the Stanislaus River has been saved from damming several times at the eleventh hour. Should the Eel in Northern California be preserved as a wild river and left in its natural state for future generations to enjoy? Or should it be dammed to prevent the river's almost yearly rampages and to supply water for people?

Ways are being considered to increase the flow of the Colorado River. Experiments are currently being done with cloud seeding to produce more precipitation, and this means more runoff for the river to carry. A proposal has been made to send the Columbia south to supplement the flow of the Colorado. This is a very controversial issue, supported by those who would benefit from more water in the Colorado. People living in the Northwest resent the idea of sharing their great natural resource with the Southwest.

Perhaps a burning question of the future is this: to whom do the rivers belong? To all people or to those who can benefit from some direct control of the waterways? The decision won't be easy.

When you defile the pleasant streams . . .
You massacre a million dreams . . . John Drinkwater

Rafting to cycling—you can enjoy a river any number of ways. Perhaps the most dedicated river recreationalists are the fishermen and white-water enthusiasts. But scores of others partake in river fun, whether swimming or inner-tubing in the water or camping and hiking along the river banks.

RIVER TALK

Rivers—like any other subject—have their own terminology, and the terms run the gamut from the common to the technical. Following is a list of river-related words you'll be most likely to encounter in books and conversation dealing with rivers:

Acre-foot-of-water. The amount of water needed to cover one acre to a depth of one foot. It consists of 326,000 gallons of water.

Aquifer. A subsurface layer of rock permeable by water. Although gravel, sand, sandstone, and limestone are the best conveyers of water, the bulk of the earth's rock is composed of clay, shale, and crystalline.

Bank. The slope of land bordering the river.

Basin. The region of land drained by a river and its tributaries.

Bed. The ground at the bottom of a river.

Current. The continuously downstream flow of water in a river, resulting from the tendency of water to move downhill toward sea level.

Dam. A barrier constructed of earth or man-made materials to hold back the flow of a river. Dams are generally for storage or diversion. Storage dams store water; diversion dams divert water. Usually, a diversion dam has no storage capabilities. Storage dams can serve more than one purpose.

Delta. Silt deposits, generally triangular in shape, collected at or in a river's mouth.

Drainage Basin. A large surface area whose waters are drained off into a principal river system.

Erosion. The wearing away of the earth's surface by natural forces, such as water, wind, and ice.

Estuary. The wide mouth of a river where the current meets and is influenced by the tides of the ocean.

Flood. Water flowing over normally dry land. Excess water in a river channel causes a river to overflow its banks.

Flood Plain. Lowlands bordering a river which are subject to flooding. Flood plains are composed of sediments carried by rivers and deposited on land during flooding.

Flow. The rate or volume of water passing a certain point within a certain time.

Forebay. An area in a canal upstream from a control structure from which diversions are made.

Ground Water. Subsurface water, accumulating because of seepage and returning to the surface as springs and through wells.

Headwaters. A term used in reference to the origin of a river.

Hydroelectric Power. Electricity generated by the force of water. River water stored in a reservoir is released through penstocks to spin the blades of a turbine—thus generating electrical energy.

Hydrology. The branch of physical geography concerned with the behavior of water in the atmosphere, on the surface of the earth, and underground. It is also concerned with the effects of water in terms of human activities.

Lateral. A man-made channel used to convey water from a canal to its delivery point.

Levee. An embankment built along a river for flood protection.

Mouth. A term referring to the end of a river, or the point at which one river discharges into another body of water (either a river, lake, or ocean). The mouth of the Willamette River is where it spills into the Columbia River. The mouth of the Columbia River is the Pacific Ocean. Pyramid Lake is the mouth of the Truckee.

Pollution. The contamination of water (such as from raw sewage, industrial waste), making it unfit to support many forms of life.

Rapids. Fast and agitated current.

Reaches. Term used to describe sections of a river. The upper reaches refer to the beginning of a river; the lower reaches to the final stages of a river.

Reservoir. Man-made body of water created by the damming, or the backing up, of a river.

Runoff. Water flowing in a river as a result of snow melt or heavy rains.

Sediment. Material carried and deposited by water.

Silt. Earthy sediment of fine particles of rock and soil suspended in and carried by water.

Spillway. A passageway at a dam through which excess reservoir water is released.

Spring. Underground water emerging naturally from the earth.

Surface Water. Water on the surface of land, in lakes, ponds, streams, or rivers.

Tributary. A river or stream flowing into a larger river or stream.

Watershed. An area so sloped as to drain a river and all its tributaries to a single point or particular area. An area from which a river receives its water supply.

Water Table. The upper level of a water-saturated zone extending beneath the ground to where the soil and all opening in the rocks are saturated.

White Water. Fast moving, frothy water; rapids.

THE COLUMBIA
The Most Water

TED STRESHINSKY

RIVER BASIN in the West

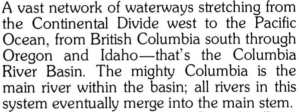

Confluence of the Willamette and Columbia rivers

A vast network of waterways stretching from the Continental Divide west to the Pacific Ocean, from British Columbia south through Oregon and Idaho—that's the Columbia River Basin. The mighty Columbia is the main river within the basin; all rivers in this system eventually merge into the main stem.

Primary supporters of the Columbia River are the systems of the Kootenai, Pend Oreille, Spokane, Wenatchee, Yakima, Willamette, Deschutes, John Day, and Snake. All together they drain 259,000 square miles.

Although each river cuts its own path and displays its own personality, their common characteristic is lots of water. Rain and snow are primary feeders of rivers, and healthy quantities of each fall in the Northwest.

Throughout the basin, the terrain varies—from forested mountains to lava plateaus to valleys. Few cities are riverfront communities. Major Oregon cities line the Willamette; in Washington, the city of Spokane straddles the Spokane River.

Unique to the Columbia River Basin are the variety of river boats traveling the system. Ocean-going vessels ply the lower Columbia and Willamette; barges and tugs work the Willamette, Snake, Columbia, St. Joe, and Coeur d' Alene. Pleasure boats ply almost every river within the basin.

In the Columbia's system, almost every river has been dammed—either for hydroelectric power, irrigation, or flood control. A few rivers, such as the Salmon's Middle Fork and St. Joe, still flow freely.

(For a map of the Columbia River Basin and its relation to the rest of the West, turn to either the inside front or back cover.)

THE COLUMBIA RIVER
Powerhouse of the West

Running 1,270 miles from Canada to the sea, the Columbia is a hard worker — producing power, irrigating lands, serving as a water highway

The Columbia is often referred to as the Mighty or Great River of the West. For it is the largest producer of water power in North America—is the West's major salmon producing stream, irrigates more land in the West than any other river, and is a major river highway. Its waters are even put to use at the atomic energy plant at Hanford Works and at the nuclear Trojan Plant.

The Columbia travels 1,270 miles from the forested slopes of the Canadian Rockies' Columbia Lake, south through eastern Washington, west through the Cascades, and out to the Pacific Ocean. Its first 500 miles are in Canada; its final 300 miles form the Washington and Oregon border.

Although the Columbia is long—second longest in the West—few cities lie along its path. Washington's Tri-cities (Kennewick, Pasco, Richland) form the major metropolitan area. Bridges span the water at Astoria, Longview, Vancouver, Hood River, The Dalles, Tri-cities, Vantage, and Grand Coulee. Small ferries cross the river at four places.

The Columbia is not only long but also wide. Eleven dams have made the river placid, appearing more like a lake than a river. Gone are the roaring rapids that challenged the dugout canoes and the skills of Lewis and Clark. Gone are the breathtaking Celilo Falls, Indian fishing grounds inundated by The Dalles Dam.

Evidence of the old Columbia does remain. Rock formations in the Columbia Gorge tell the story of the erosive action of the river and the uplifting of the Cascade Range that took place 30 million years ago. In the Columbia Basin, deep channels cut by the ancient river recall the Ice Age.

Beacon Rock, rising 848 feet above the Gorge of the Columbia, is one of the most prominent landmarks along this section of the river. Although its sheer escarpments look impossible to climb, an hour's hike along suspended walkways leads to the summit and superb views.

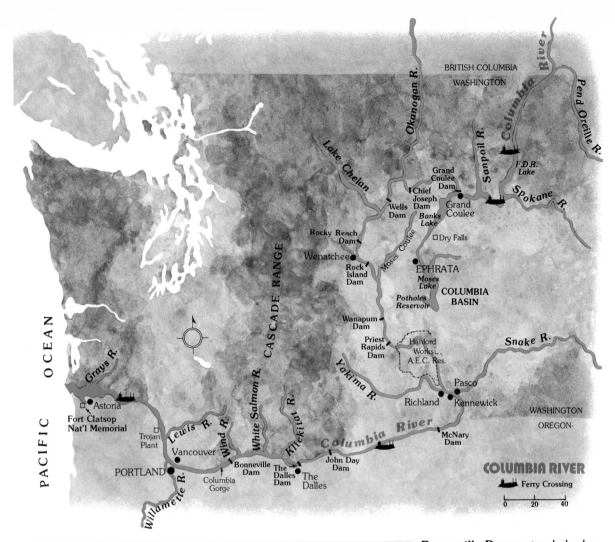

BRITISH COLUMBIA
WASHINGTON

Columbia River
Pend Oreille R.
Okanogan R.
Sanpoil R.
Spokane R.
F.D.R. Lake
Grand Coulee Dam
Chief Joseph Dam
Grand Coulee
Banks Lake
Wells Dam
Lake Chelan
Rocky Reach Dam
Moses Coulee
☐ Dry Falls
Wenatchee
Rock Island Dam
EPHRATA
Moses Lake
COLUMBIA BASIN
Potholes Reservoir
Wanapum Dam
Priest Rapids Dam
Hanford Works A.E.C. Res.
Snake R.
Yakima R.
Pasco
Richland
Kennewick
WASHINGTON
OREGON
Grays R.
Lewis R.
Wind R.
White Salmon R.
Klickitat R.
Columbia River
McNary Dam
Astoria
Fort Clatsop Nat'l Memorial
Trojan Plant
Vancouver
PORTLAND
Willamette R.
Bonneville Dam
The Dalles Dam
The Dalles
John Day Dam
Columbia Gorge
PACIFIC OCEAN
CASCADE RANGE

COLUMBIA RIVER

⬛ Ferry Crossing

0   20   40

Bonneville Dam not only looks busy, it is busy. Transmission equipment atop the powerhouse is sending energy throughout the Northwest, while a navigation lock opens to permit upstream passage of a tug. Bonneville is the oldest major dam on the Columbia (1933) and the lowest geographically.

TED STRESHINSKY

Columbia River Basin   17

Early Explorations

Beaver fever and the Columbia was mapped

First sighted and recorded in 1792 by Bostonian Robert Gray on a foray for sea otters, the Columbia River was named after the Captain's ship—Columbia Rediviva. President Thomas Jefferson, his eye on the Pacific trade and on the Canadian and British beaver trapping business in the northern Rockies, dispatched Meriwether Lewis and William Clark in 1804 to map an inland water route to the Pacific Ocean. They followed the Missouri River, portaged its Great Falls, crossed the hazardous Bitterroots, and then traveled down the Clearwater, Snake, and Columbia rivers until in Clark's journal was recorded "Ocian in view! O! the joy."

BOB WATERMAN

Fort Clatsop, built of the "streightest & most butifullest logs" was winter headquarters for Lewis and Clark in 1805-1806. Although the explorers first sighted the ocean from the storm-battered north side, they crossed to the south bank of the Columbia where salt and game were plentiful. Rain and influenza plagued the men, but they had wood and food. The explorers made friends with the Clatsops, named the fort in their honor, and, when the expedition left in the spring, turned the fort over to the local Indians. Nothing remains of the original structure. The present fort was constructed on the original site, according to descriptions in Clark's journal. A national monument, Fort Clatsop is 4½ miles southwest of Astoria.

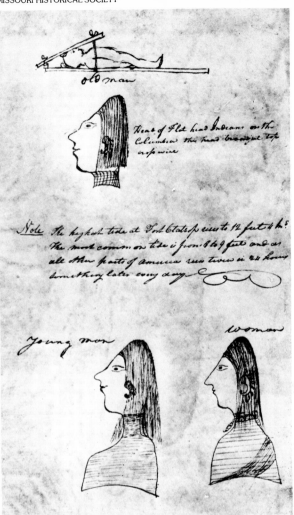

Cedar-carved canoe is a replica of the type used by the Lewis and Clark expedition west of the Rockies. Carved according to information in Clark's journal, the canoe sits at the water's edge at Fort Clatsop National Monument.

The flat look. According to Captain Clark's journal, the Indians living along the Columbia River placed infants' heads in a cradle-type apparatus, creating flat faces. In the middle of the page, Clark comments on the tides at Fort Clatsop.

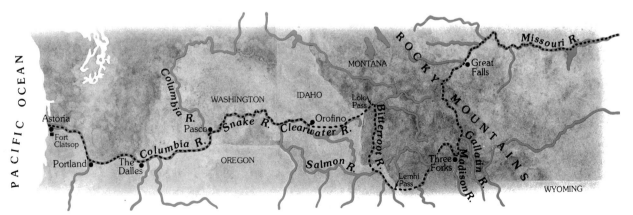

Lewis and Clark route west of the Rocky Mountains. Dotted line indicates the path the expedition took west. On May 14, 1804, Lewis and Clark left St. Louis, journeying up the Missouri River. After crossing the rugged Bitterroots, they returned to the water, canoeing down the Clearwater, Snake, and Columbia rivers.

Columbia River Basin   19

The Columbia River
Dammed for Power
Turning river current into electric current

Catching and conserving the flow of the mighty Columbia
are, from west to east, Bonneville, The Dalles, John Day,
McNary, Priest Rapids, Wanapum, Rock Island, Rocky
Reach, Wells, Chief Joseph, and Grand Coulee dams. The
main purpose of these eleven is the production of
hydroelectric power. Spring runoff, stored in reservoirs
behind each dam, is released through penstocks to turn the
turbines and generate electricity for homes and industry in
the Pacific Northwest.

Rocky Reach Dam, spanning the Columbia 11 miles north of Wenatchee, provides low-cost hydroelectric power for irrigation pumping, homes, and industry. Owned by the Chelan County Public Utility District, Rocky Reach is one of the newer dams on the Columbia, in operation since 1962. This view of Rocky Reach faces north, looking at the front of the dam. The powerhouse sits on the left. The spillway, not in operation here, runs only in summer during years of excess water.

...DAMMED FOR POWER

Spun by the force of water, turbines, enclosed in spiral casings, generate electrical energy. Although the number of turbines at each dam varies, the basic design and operation remain the same. These are housed at Bonneville.

TED STRESHINSKY

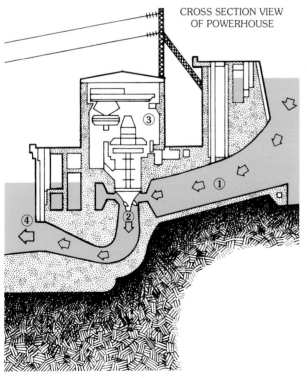

CROSS SECTION VIEW
OF POWERHOUSE

Speeding electrical energy from the hydroelectric plant to its final destination is a system of power lines. At the point of creation, electricity is too high in voltage for industrial and private purposes. Through a series of transformations, voltage is reduced to the usable 440, 220, and 110.

Hydroelectric power in 4 steps. 1) Reservoir water, having dropped hundreds of feet inside a penstock, enters powerhouse. 2) Water under tremendous pressure strikes blades of turbine, causing the turbine and the generator connected to it to spin. The generator converts water power into electric power. 3) Generated electricity goes to a transformer, and, via transmission lines, power is carried to where it is needed. 4) Water continues its flow downstream.

Salmon-Dedicated River Runners
Downstream to feed, upstream to breed

Lewis and Clark, traveling down the Columbia in the fall of 1805, found salmon "jumping very thick." Since explorer days the migratory habits of the salmon haven't changed, but the character of the river—the West's major salmon producing stream—has. Eleven dams block not only the river but also the upstream/downstream path of the fish. Damming has also meant lost spawning grounds. At the dams, fish ladders aid salmon across, and hatcheries compensate for the lost gravel beds. But salmon caught in spillways are weakened from nitrogen supersaturation; those caught in turbine blades lose their life.

Numbers game. Counting stations identify and record the fish as they swim upstream over the dam. During the past 30 years or so, more than 620,000 salmon and steelhead have passed through Bonneville (shown here), the heaviest activity occurring during the spring Chinook runs. Salmon travel as far up the Columbia as Chief Joseph Dam, 545 miles from the river's mouth. On their upstream flight, they undergo a physical change, the male more so than the female.

TED STRESHINSKY

Fish ladders, such as this one at Bonneville, enable salmon to swim over dams to reservoir water. A fish ladder (see illustration **below**) is essentially an inclined flume, 24 to 40 feet wide. A series of weirs within the flume create successive pools, each one foot higher than the preceding one. Because jumping injures salmon, water flowing down the ladder and openings 2 feet square in each partition encourage fish to swim, rather than jump, from pool to pool.

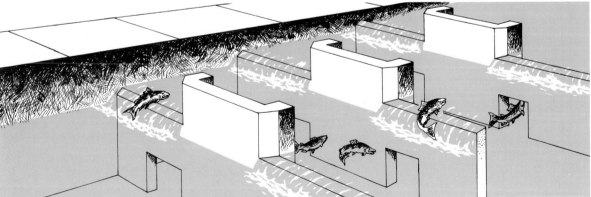

...SALMON-DEDICATED RIVER RUNNERS

BOB WATERMAN

The amateurs. *Bank fishermen cast for salmon on the Columbia River near its mouth. Since salmon do not feed as they swim upstream, the best lure is a spinner or wobbler, which will attract their attention, anger them, and cause them to lunge for it.*

BOB WATERMAN

The pros. *Commercial fisherman unloads his catch at Astoria. Salmon fishing is an important industry in the Pacific Northwest, with the commercial catch in the ocean off the coast of Washington and Oregon valued at $150 million annually.*

LIFE CYCLE OF THE SALMON

Although Pacific salmon spend most of their lives in salt water, they begin and end life and give birth to new life in fresh water. Born in gravel beds of rivers, the fingerlings travel downstream to the Pacific Ocean where they grow to maturity. At spawning time (two to five years later), the silvery fish begin the long upstream journey home to spawn and die. Their sexual maturation causes a physical change. Salmon lose weight, their silvery color turns darker, and the male develops a hooked jaw and fighting teeth. On their upstream flight, salmon consume a tremendous amount of energy swimming against the current.

Since dams on rivers present obstructions to the migrations of the salmon, numerous hatcheries have been established near dams to help control their population. At hatcheries, the salmon remain in holding ponds until ripe and are then artificially spawned. Eggs stripped from the females are fertilized. Since salmon always die after spawning—getting ready to spawn creates a physiological degenerative process in their organs that reaches its peak after the eggs are fertilized—the adult salmon are killed. Eggs hatch in incubators 50 to 60 days later, and the fingerlings live in ponds (up to 18 months of the salmon's life cycle) until they are released into the rivers to migrate downstream.

The natural spawning cycle finds the salmon depositing their eggs in gravel nests in the fall, the adults dying, and the fry hatching in spring. The embryo develops on a yolk sac (an extension of the digestive tract), and after the fry absorb the yolk sac, they work their way out of the gravel and begin their downstream voyage to the sea.

Why salmon return to their birthplace to spawn and die is a wonder of nature, though scientific evidence points to an acute sense of smell.

Steelhead trout follow the salmon migration pattern with one exception—they do not die after spawning. Steelhead may migrate five times.

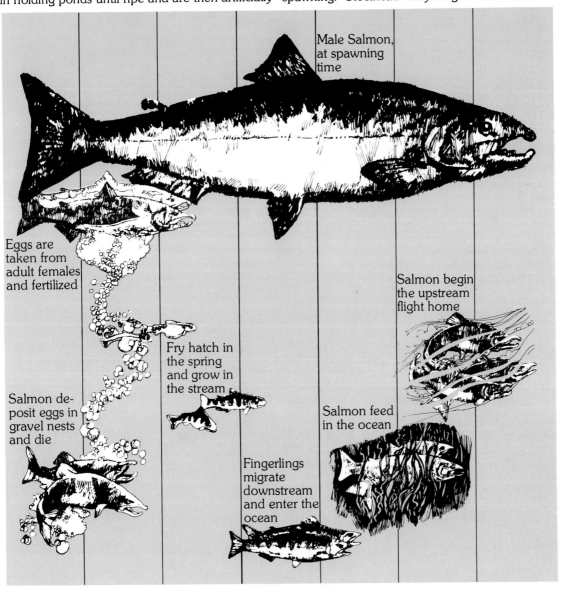

Male Salmon, at spawning time

Eggs are taken from adult females and fertilized

Salmon begin the upstream flight home

Fry hatch in the spring and grow in the stream

Salmon deposit eggs in gravel nests and die

Salmon feed in the ocean

Fingerlings migrate downstream and enter the ocean

Traffic on the Water Highway
Some boats push or pull; a few move with the wind

Almost any kind of boat—from pleasure craft to seaworthy vessel—can be seen on the Columbia. Ocean-going ships ply the river between its mouth and its meeting with the Willamette. Tugs push or pull their loads between Astoria and the Tri-cities—the Columbia's highest point of navigation. Although dams have blocked the ship's highway, locks permit river traffic to pass through the barriers and continue up or downstream. Fishing boats concentrate in the Astoria area, whereas pleasure boats are found mainly on the reservoirs. Ferries cross in four places—at Westport, Arlington, and twice within Franklin D. Roosevelt National Recreation Area.

BOB WATERMAN

RAY ATKESON

An assortment of river boats ply the Columbia. Freighters from foreign ports unload or load their cargo at one of the ports on the Columbia River or at the Port of Portland on the Willamette. Freighter **(above)** heads west under the Astoria bridge with a shipful of lumber. Ferries cross the Columbia in four spots. A free ferry **(right)** is the connecting link for Washington State Highway 21 east of Grand Coulee. Other three crossings are at Gifford, Arlington, and Westport. Sailboats **(left)** like to negotiate the river at Astoria, Hood River, and Vancouver.

Busy little tugboats either push or pull their load up or downstream. Logs and petroleum usually go up river; grain generally comes down.

Through the locks at the dams. Upstream gate opens; downstream gate closes; tug enters lock **(right).** Upstream gate closes; lock is gradually emptied to river level **(middle right).** Downstream gate opens; tug leaves lock at river level **(far right).** For upstream passage, the procedure is just reversed.

...TRAFFIC ON THE WATER HIGHWAY

TED STRESHINSKY

TED STRESHINSKY

Log Moving calls for manual and mechanical skill

Log maneuvering takes place on the Columbia, Willamette, St. Joe, and Lewis and Clark rivers and at several ports on the Columbia and one on the Willamette. Whenever possible, logs are stored in the river—storage cost is low, and water preserves the quality of the wood—and moved on the water highway. Bronco boats and men with poles direct the logs into bundles and rafts. Tugs arrive when it's time for towing. Logs go either downstream or upstream, to the mills for processing or to ports for exporting.

Bronco boats (above) move about bundles of logs being stored in the Lewis and Clark River. *Sure footing (right)* is a necessity when moving the gigantic logs individually.

Hoisting logs from river to ship takes place at several ports on the Columbia and at the Port of Portland on the Willamette. Sturdy men attach sturdy cables around logs *(top)*. Man on ship gives the signal for the crane to begin lifting *(above)*. While bundle is in the air, about to be taken aboard ship, another awaits its turn *(above right)*. Crane *(right)* is just about to deposit logs in the hull of the ship.

Columbia River Basin   33

The Columbia Gorge

Trails, waterfalls, and a riverside drive

For 60 miles (from Troutdale, east of Portland, to The Dalles), the Columbia moves through a wide, natural barrier in the Cascades. River-front drives and several overlooks on both the Oregon and Washington sides provide excellent views of the river's most scenic stretch. Geology buffs will find the gorge fascinating. Walls, in some places 2,000 feet thick, are of Columbia River basalt, formed 20 million years ago. For a closer look at the cliffs, canyons, and waterfalls—products of uplifting basalt layers and river erosion—take back-country hikes in Mt. Hood National Forest.

BOB WATERMAN

Wilderness at the highway's door. *Along the Columbia River Scenic Highway and I80 are Latourell Falls and Oneonta Gorge, two of the most impressive stops in the Columbia Gorge. Latourell Falls **(right)** drops a sheer 250 feet over basalt. The waterfall at the end of Oneonta Gorge **(above)** is not as dramatic as the route to it. Path is simply the clear but rock-studded streambed, passable only during low water in late summer. Hikers step gingerly on exposed boulders and, where the rocks are submerged, wade or scramble along the gorge's rocky walls.*

Hudson of the West. Slow and wide is the Columbia River as it moves through the Cascade Range. Looking upstream, Washington is on the north, Oregon the south. Vista House marks Crown Point, one of the best spots for an overall view of the Columbia Gorge.

The Columbia River
Coulee Country
Twice dammed...first by ice, second by concrete

During the Ice Age, huge sheets of ice—some up to 4,000 feet thick—blocked the flow of the Columbia River, forcing it to alter its course. Torrents of water raced south, cutting two coulees, or deep gorges, that were left high and dry when the glaciers receded and the river returned to its original course. Thousands of years later, in 1933, work began on the second damming of the Columbia. Grand Coulee Dam, key to the Columbia Basin Project, conserves water for ultimately irrigating 1 million acres of dry earth in eastern Washington. With completion of the third power plant in the mid 1970s, Grand Coulee will be the world's largest producer of hydroelectric power.

RAY ATKESON

Evidence of the river's two dammings are Banks Lake **(left)** and Dry Falls **(below)**. Banks Lake and Franklin D. Roosevelt Lake, created by the Columbia Basin Project, provide water-oriented recreation in the eastern Washington desert. Banks Lake is an equalizing reservoir; Roosevelt Lake, stretching 151 miles behind Grand Coulee Dam to the Canadian border, is the main water storage facility for the Project. Eerie Dry Falls, 400 feet high and 3¼ miles across, is a lingering ghost of the past when immense glaciers moved down from the north and forced the Columbia temporarily to change its course. Also in evidence at Dry Falls are layers of basalt from repeated lava flows.

How coulees were formed. 1) Twenty million years ago, the Columbia swept through central Washington, probably following a course similar to this. 2) Fifteen million years ago, repeated lava floods covered central Washington, forcing the river around the lava fields. 3) About a million years ago, vast sheets of ice moved south, blocking the Columbia and forcing its waters to cut new channels across the lava fields. 4) Today, the water-eroded coulee country. Twelve thousand years ago, the last glaciers melted, and the river returned to its old course, leaving vast scars across the lava fields in the form of coulees, dry falls, and water-eroded scablands.

Columbia River Basin 37

720,000 gallons *of water a minute—that's the carry-ing capacity of each of the six pipes at Grand Coulee Dam. At irrigation time (May to September), the six pipes lift the water 280 feet over the wall of the dam. Water is then channeled (2,000 miles of canals traverse the Columbia Basin) through the barren lava country to fields where sprinklers water the crops.*

Vivid example of irrigation benefits is evidenced by neglected sagebrush country bordering lush farmlands. Of the 2 million acres in the Columbia Basin Project area, only 1 million lend themselves to irrigation. About 500,000 acres are now under cultivation, producing crops, such as alfalfa, hay, potatoes, sugar beets, field corn, seed crops, and vegetable crops for freezing and processing.

WILLIAM A. PEDERSEN

THE SPOKANE & PEND OREILLE
In a Land of Lakes, Some Rivers too

Sometimes working, sometimes offering pleasure, the Spokane and Pend Oreille river systems traverse country from western Montana to eastern Washington

Mention Spokane and city comes to mind. Mention Pend Oreille and lake comes to mind. But Spokane and Pend Oreille are also rivers, which, along with their tributaries, drain an area from Montana to eastern Washington.

The Spokane's system begins in the Bitterroot Range with the St. Joe and Coeur d'Alene rivers. West they flow until they spill into Coeur d'Alene Lake. Out of Coeur d'Alene Lake pours the Spokane River.

The Pend Oreille originates in the Rockies, with the Clark Fork moving west to Pend Oreille Lake. From Pend Oreille Lake emerges the Pend Oreille River.

The lakes in Idaho's panhandle attract the outdoorsman. But rivers offer recreation too. Spots on the Spokane, Priest, Coeur d'Alene, Pend Oreille, and St. Joe rivers are perfect for rafting, tubing, canoeing, and fly fishing. In Spokane's Riverside Park, lava formations sit in the middle of the Spokane River, picnic grounds border the banks, and a footbridge spans the water.

More important than pleasure is the job the rivers perform. Six dams on the Spokane and 12 on the Pend Oreille's system provide energy for the immediate area and for Seattle. The free-flowing Coeur d'Alene and St. Joe serve as a highway for transporting logs.

Use of these rivers for a highway dates back to explorer days. After the pathfinder came fur trappers, mountain men, missionaries, and settlers. Of all the early settlements that were established alongside the river, only one—Spokane—has emerged as a major metropolitan area. Many small communities lie along the river banks, while highways follow and cross the rivers.

The leisurely river. The Pend Oreille River drifts past a farmhouse settled down for the winter just outside Metaline Falls, Washington. For most of its way, the Pend Oreille flows through agricultural valleys bordered by forested slopes.

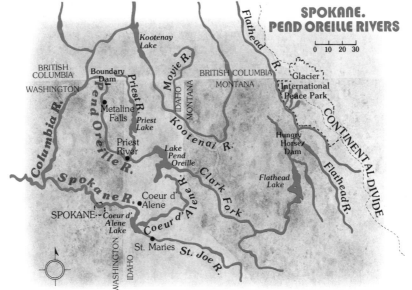

SPOKANE, PEND OREILLE RIVERS

0 10 20 30

Kootenay Lake

Flathead R.

BRITISH COLUMBIA
WASHINGTON

Boundary Dam

Pend Oreille R.

Priest R.

Moyie R.

BRITISH COLUMBIA
MONTANA

Glacier International Peace Park

Columbia R.

Metaline Falls

Priest Lake

Priest River

IDAHO
MONTANA

Kootenai R.

Lake Pend Oreille

Hungry Horse Dam

CONTINENTAL DIVIDE

Flathead Lake

Flathead R.

Spokane R.

Clark Fork

Coeur d' Alene

SPOKANE

Coeur d' Alene Lake

Coeur d' Alene R.

St. Maries

St. Joe R.

WASHINGTON
IDAHO

The working river. Control gates of Upriver Dam east of downtown Spokane release Spokane River water. Owned by the city of Spokane, Upriver Dam produces energy for the metropolitan area.

Columbia River Basin 41

The Coeur d'Alene, St. Joe, and Priest
In Idaho's Panhandle
Lumbering...big business, big pleasure

Since the turn of the century, the St. Joe and Coeur d'Alene rivers have played an active role in the moving of logs across Idaho's panhandle. Stands of timber, harvested in the St. Joe and Coeur d'Alene national forests, are trucked or railroaded to the river and dumped into the water. Logs are put in bundles, bundles are made into rafts, and rafts are towed downstream to the sawmills on the north side of Coeur d'Alene Lake. A low-cost method of storing and moving logs, tows take place from June to March when ice forms on the rivers and lake.

WILLIAM A. PEDERSEN

WILLIAM A. PEDERSEN

Axe thrower (above), pole climber (right), wood chopper (below) gather at annual loggers' festival in Priest River on the Priest River to display their skills.

WILLIAM A. PEDERSEN

One of the last rivers to serve as a highway for log tows, the St. Joe (here in the vicinity of St. Maries) conveys logs from the forests to Coeur d'Alene for processing. About 120 million board feet of logs come down the river annually.

The Spokane, Pend Oreille, Coeur d'Alene, Clark Fork, Priest, and St. Joe
River Recreation
A wilderness of opportunities

Rivers in the Spokane/Pend Oreille system take a backseat to northern Idaho's lakes when it comes to recreation. And it is easy to see why. Record catches of Kamloops and Dolly Varden attract fishermen, and miles of flat water appeal to water-skiers and boaters. But these same sports can be enjoyed on the river. Fly fishermen should have luck in the Coeur d'Alene, Spokane, Pend Oreille, Clark Fork, and Priest rivers. Power boats can negotiate the St. Joe and Pend Oreille rivers. Innertubing is safe along sections of the Spokane, Coeur d'Alene, and Pend Oreille rivers.

Nature's roller coaster. Many stretches of the Spokane River in Spokane provide a safe and exciting raft ride. But the uninitiated should avoid the spots where the current is extremely rough. Two tough stretches are around the massive lava formations ("Bowl and Pitcher") in Riverside State Park and "Toenail" rapids. Calm water flows around Glover Field.

Record catches of Kamloops and Dolly Varden make northern Idaho's lakes famous fishing grounds. But fly fishing in the Clark Fork can be rewarding too.

Frothy at times and somewhat rocky, Priest River (in the vicinity of the town of Priest River) is generally good for innertubing.

Streaking the Pend Oreille River, power boaters sometimes tackle the river current, although most prefer the expansive waters of Coeur d'Alene, Pend Oreille, and Priest lakes.

Columbia River Basin   45

The Spokane in Spokane
The recognition of a river

For a hundred years, the Spokane River roared through the middle of Spokane, hidden from view by warehouses, railroad yards and trestles, and decaying structures. In the early 1960s, city planners felt it was time to bring the Spokane River out of hiding, and the eventual result was a massive beautification program in conjunction with Expo '74. The site selected for the World's Fair was 100 river-front acres and two islands—Havermale and Cannon. With an environmental theme, down went the old and up went the new. At the close of the fair in fall of 1974, buildings were dismantled, but the people of Spokane were left with a river side park and a new respect for their magnificent river.

JACK McDOWELL

STEEL

A wild river in town. Before the Spokane reaches Spokane, it wanders through flat agricultural lands. But once the river hits downtown, it crashes over three separate but consecutive falls. For a close view of the rushing waters, cross over the middle drop on a suspension footbridge (here in its final stages of construction for Expo '74) from the north bank of the river to Havermale Island.

Sight and sound of Spokane Falls is part of Spokane's downtown scene. View here is from an overlook on the south side of the river, below the Monroe Street Bridge and just off Trent Avenue.

THE YAKIMA & WENATCHEE
Heart of Apple Country

Falling fast down the forested slopes of the Cascades to the Columbia River, the Yakima and Wenatchee's main stop is the orchards of central Washington

Wilderness rivers in their beginnings, semi-arid valley rivers in their lower reaches—that's the Wenatchee and Yakima. Main tributaries to the Columbia River on the eastern side of the Cascade Range, the Yakima and Wenatchee each journey about 175 miles and fall about 7,000 feet.

Both rivers are used primarily for irrigation. Row after row of fruit trees—growing well because of a favorable climate, rich volcanic soil, and plenty of river water—cover the valley. Apples are the big crop. Wenatchee ships more apples than any other community in the world.

Neither river shines in the recreational field. Trout fishing is good in the Yakima River, and both rivers have salmon runs. At Sunnyside Dam on the Yakima River, Yakima Indians in the tradition of their ancestors dip net for salmon during spring runs. Leisurely rafting or kayaking takes place on the lower Yakima; rigorous rafting and kayaking are found on the upper Wenatchee.

The most eye-catching spot on either river is Tumwater Canyon, cut by the Wenatchee near Leavenworth. Fall brings a splendid show of color from the vine maples and sumac; spring finds the river, swollen from snow melt, a roaring cascade.

Two major cities lie along the rivers, both bearing the names of the rivers and both situated in the lower reaches: Yakima and Wenatchee. Between the Yakima and the Columbia rivers sits the 1,000,000-acre Yakima Indian Reservation.

Die-hard fishermen. *When salmon and trout fishermen have called it quits for the winter, the white fish angler takes to the river. Near Harrison Bridge in Selah (just north of Yakima), hardy souls stand in the icy waters of the Yakima River waiting for a catch.*

Unspoiled pasturelands and orchards cover the flatlands bordering the Wenatchee River. Behind them, the rounded foothills on the eastern side of the Cascade Range make a dramatic backdrop. The Yakima and Wenatchee rivers join with Lake Chelan and the Columbia River in keeping central Washington supplied with water.

The Yakima and Wenatchee
In the River Valleys
Everywhere an apple explosion

Since the early 1900s when irrigation came to central Washington, apple growing has been big business in the Yakima and Wenatchee valleys. Soil rich in volcanic ash, a dry and temperate climate, and a plentiful supply of water for irrigation from the Wenatchee and Yakima rivers and Lake Chelan provide the right combination for turning out 35 million boxes of apples each season. More apples come from Wenatchee than from any other community in the world. In May, the apple trees are covered with fragrant pink blossoms; in the fall, orchards blaze with reds and golds as the fruit ripens.

BOB WATERMAN

The "big two." Red Delicious **(above)** and Golden Delicious **(left)** are the big two of the "Big Six" varieties of Washington apples. Other four are Newton, Rome Beauty, Jonathan, and Winesap. A total of 35 million boxes of apples comes from central Washington each season.

Winding Wenatchee flows through semi-arid country in central Washington. Volcanic ash soil, a dry and temperate climate, and plenty of river water for irrigation make the perfect combination for producing orchards and orchards of fruit—especially apples.

Fifty thousand people converge on Appleland in the fall to help with the harvest. Picked by hand from the tree, the fruit is placed in a special canvas-lined bag to prevent bruising. When the bag is full, the picker releases the string, allowing the flap on the bottom of the bag to open, and gently deposits the apples in a bin. Each orchard bin holds 25 bushels.

Stacker to packer. *Tractors move through the orchards, pick up the orchard bins, and place them in rows (**above**). Then a "straddle tractor" gathers the bins and rushes the apples to cold storage. During harvest season, freshly picked apples are found at roadside stands in the apple country (**left**).*

Columbia River Basin   53

In the Higher Elevations

Reds and yellows at their splashiest!

The Yakima and Wenatchee begin as mountain rivers. Cold and fast, they emerge from the Cascades and surge with strength down the eastern slopes of the range before meeting the semi-arid valleys of central Washington. High up, a multitude of deciduous trees border the rivers, creating a colorful display in the fall when the cold temperatures cause the leaves to change color. One of the best spots in the West to sample riverside fall color is Tumwater Canyon, cut by the Wenatchee River near Leavenworth.

BOB WATERMAN

BOB WATERMAN

Autumn reflections. *Gold-yellow willows and the blazing red vine maples and sumac shimmer in the stillness of the Wenatchee River. Stands of deciduous trees, showing their most colorful side when the thermometer dips below freezing, border the upper Wenatchee and Yakima rivers. The best place to view fall color is Tumwater Canyon, on the Wenatchee River near Leavenworth. U. S. Highway 2 passes through an 8-mile section of the canyon.*

BOB WATERMAN

Columbia River Basin   55

THE WILLAMETTE RIVER
Lifeline of Oregon

In the river's valley lie the state's great agricultural and industrial resources and most of its people

In the early 1960s, the Willamette River was the most polluted river in the Pacific Northwest. For years, raw sewage and industrial waste had been dumped into the river. Into the waters the rains washed farming debris.

But the survival of the Willamette River was so crucial to Oregon, for it served 21 municipalities and 600 industries and provided water to irrigate thousands of acres of rich agricultural lands. In 1969 the Oregon legislature created the Department of Environmental Quality, which set up strict water quality rules. No longer could waste be indiscriminately discharged into public waters. Permits were required, and waste treatment standards were established. With cities and private enterprise cooperating, the Willamette flows 90 per cent cleaner today than it did a decade ago.

The Willamette begins at the merging of two streams—one from the Cascades, the other from the Coast Range. In its 255-mile journey north to the Columbia, the river flows through the fertile Willamette Valley. Along the way lie Oregon's major cities—Eugene, Corvallis, Salem (state capital), Oregon City, and Portland. Agricultural lands cover the Eugene to Salem area, whereas the Portland/Oregon City section is industrial and commercial.

From Eugene to Portland, the Willamette flows freely. Dams on the headwaters have modified the river's winter rampages.

Water traffic on the Willamette ranges from pleasure boats to commercial vessels. Upstream point of navigation for ocean-going ships is the Port of Portland, although tugs and barges can travel as far as Oregon City. At three spots, small ferries cross the river.

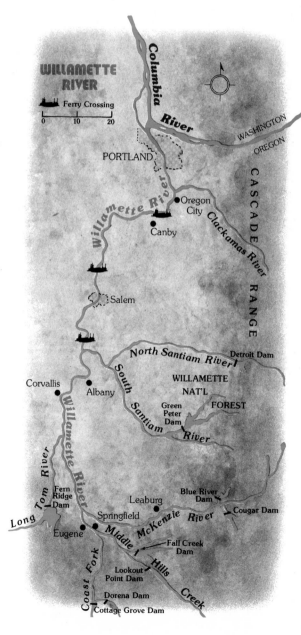

Water traffic *can be as hectic as downtown traffic where the Willamette slices through Portland. Pleasure boats travel the river from its headwaters to its mouth.*

Across the Willamette. *Three ferries—one at Canby, Buena Vista, and Wheatland—take passengers and cars from one bank to another. The Canby ferry* ***(left)*** *is powered by electricity coming from an overhead cable.*

Columbia River Basin 57

An Agricultural Empire

River + mild climate = 100 crops

Fertile soil along the Willamette, a mild climate, an average annual rainfall of 35 inches, and supplemental irrigation (280,000 acres) make the Willamette Valley agriculturally rich. More than 100 crops (among the most important are snap beans, sweet corn, strawberries, grass seed, filberts, and mint) account for 43 per cent of Oregon farm sales. Since many fruits and vegetables are grown for canning, Salem has emerged as a major food processing center. From June to September, the valley bustles with activity as workers and machines take to the fields for the harvest.

TED STRESHINSKY

Bumper crops of pole beans, grass seed, and hops are produced yearly in the Willamette Valley. Pole beans, handpicked by students in August, are sacked and then dumped into bins for weighing **(far left).** Grass seed **(left)** is harvested in midsummer, after the dry season has set in and the fields have turned a golden brown. Hops **(above),** climbing up vertical strings to high wires suspended between husky poles, like the mild winters, wet springs, and dry summers.

TED STRESHINSKY

Soil dictated by the Willamette. *The types of soil found in the Willamette Valley have been determined by the river. Floods over the centuries dropped the heavier sandy particles near the river and distributed the lighter clay soil particles farther away. Within a mile or less of the river are the richest soils which will grow any crop the climate and economy will allow. The poorest soil will support only pasture, hay, grain, and grass seed. But, no matter the soil type or crop, sometimes supplemental water is required, such as with corn, to produce the most bountiful crop.*

TED STRESHINSKY

The Willamette River

Eugene to Portland

River-oriented communities since the early 1800s

Since the 1830s when French Canadian fur trappers settled along the Willamette, the river's valley has been the pulse of Oregon. Here lies two-thirds of Oregon's population, the state's major cities, major industries, higher educational institutions, the state capital, and the West's leading fresh-water port. But having all of Oregon's action along the Willamette had a detrimental effect on the quality of the water. For years, municipalities and industries dumped waste into the river, creating serious pollution problems. Yet in less than a decade, through stringent environmental laws and the cooperation of parties involved, the Willamette has become 90 per cent pollution free.

TED STRESHINSKY

Portland's port is the destination for a load of grain pushed downstream by a tugboat *(left)*. Located on the Willamette 10 miles above its confluence with the Columbia, the Port of Portland exports regional materials—grain, logs, lumber, paper products—and loads and unloads about 2,500 deep draft vessels annually. Industry, rather than shipping, is the main activity at Oregon City *(below)*. Industrial waste, once a major pollution problem, no longer poses a threat to the river. Crown Zellerbach, for example, has constructed a $2½ million waste water treatment project at their pulp and paper mill. Eight motor driven aerators (one shown at *right*) beat oxygen back into the water before it is released into the river.

Home to the "chief." *Dr. John McLoughlin, Chief Factor of Hudson's Bay Company, claimed land along the Willamette in 1829, laid out Oregon City in 1842, and took up residence there upon retiring three years later. Although Dr. and Mrs. McLoughlin built their home on the east bank of the river at Willamette Falls, the McLoughlin House stands today on a bluff overlooking the river. It is a national historic site.*

TED STRESHINSKY

Crewing down the Willamette. *Light, fragile shells guided by oars glide silently down the Willamette River in late afternoon at Corvallis. In the fall the river is the practicing ground for the Oregon State University crew. Spring brings the racing season, with the Willamette the scene of the annual Corvallis Invitational Regatta, one of the largest in the nation. OSU also uses the river for canoeing classes. Canoes paddle the river between Corvallis and Albany and from Peoria to Corvallis.*

The Recreational Willamette

A river parkway—255 miles long

Canoers, rafters, and swimmers flock to the upper Willamette; power boaters and water-skiers ply the river between Corvallis and Oregon City. Below Oregon City, pleasure boats share the river with commercial vessels. A fair number of state parks, with picnicking facilities, trails, launching ramps, and even museums, sit alongside the river. The eventual goal of the state's greenbelt plan is a chain of parks, campsites, trails, drives, and marinas along both banks of the Willamette from south of Eugene to north of Portland.

DON NORMARK

Sailboats to outboards—all types of pleasure craft ride the Willamette. Access to the river is easy, with numerous state parks and many towns lining the banks. Along the upper Willamette, lush banks of cottonwoods and willows make good picnicking and camping sites.

Clean water, clean fun. *A former Portlander recalls recreation on the Willamette in the early 1960s. Her family was not allowed to touch the water, and, after returning home, the boat was carefully washed. With the water today running 90 per cent cleaner, the bulk of Oregon's population has within easy reach a fresh and lazy river in which to revel.*

Columbia River Basin 67

TED STRESHINSKY

TED STRESHINSKY

Return of the salmon and the fishermen. Sport fishermen proudly display their catch of spring Chinook salmon before the thundering crash of Willamette Falls at Oregon City. (Telephoto lens compresses the distance between fishermen and falls.) In the early 1960s, the Willamette River was so heavily polluted that salmon runs—especially in the fall—were practically non-existent. But, with the successful cleanup of the river, the salmon have returned to spawn. Spring migrations, heavier than those in fall, usually begin about the middle of March, peaking sometime around mid-to-late April.

The Willamette River
In Portland
Ten ways across the Willamette

With Portland sitting on both sides of the Willamette River, a drive around the city can take you time and again across one of the ten bridges that span the water. From south to north, these are the bridges: Sellwood, Ross Island, Marquam, Hawthorne, Morrison, Burnside, Steel, Broadway, Fremont, and St. John's. Hawthorne, built in 1911, is the oldest; Fremont, opened to traffic in 1974, is the newest. Each bridge has its own personality, distinguished by color, type, or size. Broadway, Steel, Burnside, Morrison, and Hawthorne are drawbridges. All crossings are free.

JACK McDOWELL

JACK McDOWELL

Stacked bridges *and freeways cross and parallel the Willamette. Since the 1850s, Portland has straddled both banks of the river, and, as the city grew, so did the need for an efficient means of moving people around it. Looking from the Burnside Bridge, this view faces Portland's western skyline.*

Wooden planks *form the pedestrian walkway on the steel Hawthorne Bridge. All but two of Portland's ten crossings have walkways. The two that don't are the Marquam and the Fremont.*

Under as well as over. *Tug moves under the Burnside Bridge, while cars speed over the water. Some of the crossings are drawbridges; if a vessel is too tall to safely clear the span, the boat and bridge signal each other and the bridge opens or lifts to allow the vessel to pass.*

Complexity *of steel bridge in background contrasts with slick, severe concrete freeways. The first steel bridge on the Pacific Coast (built in 1912), it has two levels—trains pass on the lower level, cars on the upper level.*

Ross Island Bridge *spans the river just below Ross Island. A cantilever truss structure, Ross Island is one of the seven county-owned bridges. The state owns the Marquam and the Fremont; Union Pacific Railroad owns the Steel.*

Columbia River Basin 71

Oregon's McKenzie

Heralded for its river guides, river boats, rainbow trout

Truly one of Oregon's most beautiful rivers, the McKenzie alternately moves swiftly and slowly through the timbered lands of Willamette National Forest. On its downstream journey from the Cascades to the Willamette Valley, the river is bordered mainly by firs and cedars, but color highlights the river when the deciduous trees turn in the fall and wild rhododendrons bloom in the spring. One way to enjoy the McKenzie is to fish for rainbow trout in a McKenzie River Boat piloted by a McKenzie River Guide. Another way is to simply drive U.S. Highway 126, which parallels the river its entire length from its origin at Clear Lake to its demise in the Willamette River around Eugene.

TED STRESHINSKY

TED STRESHINSKY

White-water fishing in an oar-propelled dory. Trout season on the McKenzie is May through October; salmon runs occur in May and June. Excellent for drift fishing are the McKenzie River Boats, a type of dory with upturned ends and shallow draft designed especially for use on the McKenzie River by McKenzie River Guides.

Fifty-year veteran John S. West. Boating the McKenzie is a way of life for the McKenzie River Guides, a small group of individuals who have made it their business to know the personality of the river.

Goodpasture Bridge, *welcoming vehicular traffic since 1938, spans the McKenzie River near Leaburg. Built of wood, the covered bridge has survived traffic—mostly by logging equipment—and time well.*

THE DESCHUTES & JOHN DAY
Oregon's Lonely Rivers

Journeying north the Deschutes and John Day
have sliced through layers of lava
to expose the geologic story of 30 million years ago

The Deschutes River surges full and fast from the Cascades, whereas the John Day River comes from snow melt in eastern Oregon's Strawberry and Blue mountains. Although the John Day runs west at first, both rivers flow north to the Columbia River. Major highways cross the rivers, but only a few towns lie along their paths. John Day is the biggest on the John Day; Bend and The Dalles straddle the Deschutes. The Deschutes River also forms the eastern border for Warm Springs Indian Reservation. And their lower reaches are classified as scenic waterways by Oregon.

Being on the eastern side of the Cascades, central Oregon is semi arid. Some dry farming takes place, but, wherever possible, irrigation is used. Round Butte Dam blocks the Deschutes, Metolius, and Crooked rivers where the three meet, creating rich agricultural land. Rangelands in the Crooked River and John Day valleys abound.

Recreational activities vary—from rafting the lower Deschutes to rock hounding around Prineville. The Deschutes National Forest has hiking trails, campsites, and excellent fishing; reservoirs on the Deschutes and Crooked rivers offer boating and fishing.

But the real magic of the Deschutes and John Day rivers rests in their geologic history. Along the John Day River are fossil beds revealing specimens that roamed the valley 30 million years ago. In Smith Rock State Park, sedimentary rock formations stand above hardened layers of lava deposited during the great Columbia lava flow. And at Cove Palisades State Park, ancient sands hold a variety of minerals, and volcanic debris is eroded into sharp cliffs.

JOHN DAY,
DESCHUTES RIVERS

0   10   20

BOB WATERMAN

River crossings depend on the river. At one spot along the John Day River—near the river's mouth and east of Wasco—you can ford the water **(left)** just as the pioneers did on the Oregon Trail. Any vehicle with reasonably high clearance should be able to make it across the rubble-bottomed riffle 100 feet wide. To cross the Crooked River at its gorge, you must do so 304 feet above the river bed. The bridge spanning the 400-foot-wide canyon and the overlook **(above)** are at Ogden Scenic Wayside.

Geology on View
When rivers ran with lava

About 50 million years ago, eastern Oregon was a region of lakes. The Cascade hills were green with forests and colorful with flowering plants. But the inner forces of the earth were at work, and this idyllic scene was to be erased forever from the land. Vast flows of lava, known today as the great Columbia lava flow, began to upwell from the earth. From hills poured gigantic rivers of molten rock, filling in lakes and valleys to the east, surrounding high mountain peaks with a sea of basalt, and forming the great plateau that covers central Oregon. Evidence of this volcanic action can be seen along the Deschutes and John Day rivers where they have sliced their way through central Oregon.

BOB WATERMAN

In prehistoric times *as many as 25 lava flows moved through the lower Deschutes Valley. After the volcanic activity quieted down, the Deschutes, Metolius, and Crooked rivers began to grind their way through the layers of lava, leaving them exposed to view. At Cove Palisades State Park, lava canyon walls mirroring in the clear waters of Lake Chinook recall the earth's more turbulent days.*

Smith Rock, *part of the ancient John Day Formation, towers above the Crooked River, the flat farmlands, and the lava plains. Around the rock are rhyolite and tuffa, remains of later lava flows. The rocks tilt to the southeast. On the north bank of the river is a high rim of basalt; on the south bank are weather-eroded pinnacles.*

The Deschutes, Crooked, and Metolius
Along the Deschutes
A varied path and personality

Between its headwaters in the Cascades and the town of Warm Springs, the Deschutes River flows through accessible and quiet country. In Deschutes National Forest, the river is an excellent trout-fishing stream. In Bend, residences and city parks lie along the river banks. On Lake Chinook (which is the reservoir behind Round Butte Dam and the merging point of the Deschutes, Metolius, and Crooked rivers) are miles of water for fishing and pleasure boating. Below Warm Springs the Deschutes changes it pace, plunging largely through roadless terrain. The lower Deschutes has been designated a state scenic waterway by Oregon.

Dip netting for salmon, Indians stand on platforms overhanging the Deschutes and swing their nets through the water. Near Maupin the frothy Deschutes churns wildly through the barren countryside of northcentral Oregon.

SALLY E. KISTLER

BOB WATERMAN

Life in Bend. Since the Deschutes travels right through town, residents as well as ducks have a chance to live on the river. If you don't have a home on the water, you can visit Drake or Pioneer parks, city-owned acres of green bordering the river.

Recreation before the ages. *Cove Palisades State Park is a good launching point for fishing or boating Lake Chinook, the irrigation reservoir behind Round Butte Dam. No matter where you are on Lake Chinook, the geological history of eastern Oregon is exposed to you in the layers of lava seemingly etched in the canyon walls.*

A scenic waterway *from below Pelton Dam to its mouth, the Deschutes River whips through remote areas unreachable by roads. Organized one-man raft trips usually travel the "wild" Deschutes during spring and early summer, when the river runs full of water.*

The Peaceful Countryside
Cattle range where rhinos once roamed

Throughout the relatively unpeopled John Day Valley, beef cattle ranching is a big industry. But the cattle that now dot the landscape are a marked contrast to the camels, rhinoceroses, elephants, and now-extinct animals who made the valley their home 30 million years ago. In the 1880s, Thomas Condon discovered fossil beds along the John Day River that yielded the identity of Oregon's "early" characters. For a close up view of the fossils, visit Thomas Condon John Day Fossil Beds State Park and scout the area around Dayville.

BOB WATERMAN

Herds of cattle *graze undisturbed around the town of John Day* ***(left)*** *and in the shadow of Smith Rock in the Crooked River Valley* ***(below)***. *Both areas lie in semi-arid central Oregon, but the lands along the Crooked River are always green, even during irrigation season. Horses pasture in the Crooked River Canyon, a tranquil scene compared to those of prehistoric times, when now-extinct animals roamed the range.*

BOB WATERMAN

Western Rivers...where they begin and end

Where from, where to? Natural, free-flowing bodies of water, rivers come from rain, snow, underground springs, and glaciers. Rain and snow are the main contributors, and, for that reason, the greatest concentration of rivers and the heaviest flows lie in the Pacific Northwest. The smallest number of rivers flow in the Great Basin—an area of little moisture. All rivers eventually reach the sea, except those in the Great Basin which, because of evaporation, simply disappear. On occasion, rivers begin and end in lakes.

BOB WATERMAN

ED COOPER

KEITH GUNNAR

BOB WATERMAN

Sinks and seas are the natural endings for a river. Although rivers within a system merge into one another, eventually the main stem empties into the ocean. Rivers in the Great Basin are the exception, drying up before reaching their terminal point. Waterless Owens Lake **(left)** is the mouth of the Owens River. Washington's Hoh River **(below)** is about to enter the Pacific Ocean.

Primary chargers of rivers are rain and snow. Unusual changes in the annual rainfall or in the moisture content of snow can alter greatly a river's water level. Less frequent sources of rivers are glaciers (at **far left** is the snout of Carbon Glacier in Mt. Rainier National Park) and underground springs (at **left** is Oregon's Metolius River, which has just surfaced).

Columbia River Basin   83

THE SNAKE RIVER
Once the "Accursed Mad River"

Flowing from the Divide to the Columbia River, the Snake—still scenic and rugged in places—has largely been tamed by dams built along its 1,038-mile route

Rising at the top of the Continental Divide, the Snake River flows south through Wyoming, west across southern Idaho, and then north, forming the Idaho/Oregon border and the Idaho/Washington border before turning west to empty into the Columbia River.

Because the river covers so much territory on its 1,038-mile journey, it traverses a wide variety of terrain. In its upper reaches, it meanders through mountains. Across Idaho it cuts through lava plateaus. As it swings north, it churns through the deepest gorge on the North American continent. When it turns west into Washington, the countryside begins to flatten out.

The Snake fits quite easily into two categories: scenic and working, with the majority of the river falling into the working class. From the time the Snake enters Idaho until its demise in the Columbia, it is tapped for hydroelectric power and for irrigation. With completion of the deep-water channel to Lewiston in 1975, the Snake will serve commercial water traffic. The scenic stretches are in the Teton area and through Hells Canyon.

How to enjoy the Snake depends on where you are. From Palisades Reservoir in eastern Idaho to Lake Sacajawea in eastern Washington, reservoirs provide the usual boating, water-skiing, and fishing opportunities. In the Tetons and in Hells Canyon, you can boat and fish the river.

With the exception of Hells Canyon, which is reached only by boat or trail, the Snake is paralleled by or is close to major highways. Cities along the Snake include Jackson, Wyoming, and Twin Falls, Idaho Falls, Pocatello, Boise, and Lewiston, Idaho.

ED COOPER

Resembling a dropped handkerchief, *the glaciated peak of Mt. Moran reflects in the Snake River at Oxbow Bend in Grand Teton National Park.*

The Snake shows off. *Controlled by dams throughout the Snake River Plain, the river occasionally has a chance to show its dramatic side. At Shoshone Falls, the Snake plunges 212 feet over a 1,000-foot-wide, horseshoe-shaped basalt rim.*

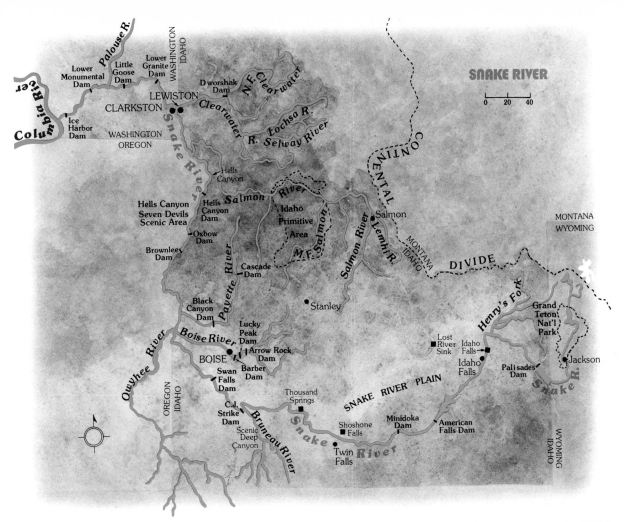

Palouse R.

Columbia River

Lower Monumental Dam

Little Goose Dam

Lower Granite Dam

WASHINGTON
IDAHO

LEWISTON

CLARKSTON

Ice Harbor Dam

Dworshak Dam

N.F. Clearwater

Clearwater R.

Lochsa R.

Selway River

WASHINGTON
OREGON

Snake River

Hells Canyon

Hells Canyon Seven Devils Scenic Area

Hells Canyon Dam

Salmon River

Idaho Primitive Area

M.F. Salmon

Salmon

Oxbow Dam

Brownlee Dam

Payette River

Cascade Dam

Salmon River

Lemhi R.

MONTANA
IDAHO

DIVIDE

CONTINENTAL

MONTANA
WYOMING

Black Canyon Dam

Stanley

Henry's Fork

Grand Teton Nat'l Park

Boise River

Lucky Peak Dam

Arrow Rock Dam

BOISE

Lost River Sink

Idaho Falls

Palisades Dam

Jackson

Ouyhee River

Swan Falls Dam

Barber Dam

Idaho Falls

Snake R.

OREGON
IDAHO

C.J. Strike Dam

Thousand Springs

SNAKE RIVER PLAIN

American Falls Dam

Scenic Deep Canyon

Bruneau River

Snake

Shoshone Falls

Minidoka Dam

WYOMING
IDAHO

Twin Falls

River

0   20   40

JIM POTH

The Snake River

In the Vicinity of the Tetons
Wild water...wild country...wildlife

Twisting between the towering Tetons on the west and less impressive ranges on the east, the upper Snake flows through countryside little changed from its look during the days of the fur trapper. Largely protected within the boundaries of Grand Teton National Park, the river is bordered by timber, meadows, and marsh lands that are home to a variety of wildlife. Inside the park the water appears placid, but the current is swift. Summer finds this stretch of river peopled with kayakers, rafters, canoers, and fishermen. Slightly south of the park, where the Snake cuts a spectacular 10-mile-long canyon, lies the truly rough water.

LINDA COHEN

Moose tracks and ski tracks. Cross country skiers follow the river bank, while moose, as evidenced by their tracks in the fresh snow, chose to cross the Snake's icy waters.

LINDA COHEN

Bundled in rain suits for protection against the cold spray, sightseers ride the white water in the Snake River Canyon. Because of the numerous rapids, the best way to experience the canyon is with a commercial outfitter on a half-day float trip.

The Snake River
...VICINITY OF THE TETONS

*Wily **weasel** when not looking for a handout may be found close to the Snake River pursuing field mice. In winter, when their brown backs and yellow fronts turn white, weasels become ermines.*

LINDA COHEN

LINDA COHEN

Ambling antelope *roam the wide, open meadows surrounding the Snake within Teton National Park. Herds are most likely to be seen in the summer sprinting gracefully by.*

Munching moose *is right at home in the upper Snake region. Good swimmers, moose feed mainly on willows that thrive along the river banks and inhabit swampy or forested lands. If you visit the Tetons, have binoculars, and are patient enough, you will be rewarded with long distance views of these enormous animals.*

The Snake River Plain
Water for people, power, and potatoes

As the Snake River journeys across southern Idaho, it is not the scenic river of the Teton area, nor is it the rugged river of Hells Canyon. Instead, it is a placid waterway, moving through lava plateaus. Along its generally dry and barren path, a series of dams—from Palisades in eastern Idaho to Hells Canyon on the Idaho/Oregon border—keep the Snake under control. Damming the river brings three major benefits to Idaho. From its waters come energy for Idaho communities, power to operate the electric pumps used to transfer water from the river bed to the plateaus, and water to irrigate the once barren fields.

RON COHEN

Potatoes are number one.
Volcanic soil, low humidity, cool evenings, and the availability of water for irrigation from the Snake River makes potato growing successful. Agriculture is Idaho's leading industry, and the majority of the farmlands lie in the valley of the Snake. Besides potatoes, other important crops are dry beans, sugar beets, feed crops, alfalfa seed, and wheat.

Idaho Falls in Idaho Falls.
Negotiating a low but wide drop, the Snake River moves through downtown Idaho Falls. Winter finds the river's icy waters down, exposing brush and boulders covered in spring when the Snake swells from snow melt in the Rockies. On the west bank of the river near the falls are spots for picnicking, fishing, and strolling.

RIVER NAMES— ROOTED IN HISTORY

Western rivers have carried a colorful cast of characters—Spanish explorers, who discovered inland waterways; Indians, who used the rivers for highways and as sources of food; American pathfinders and fur trappers, who opened up the West. From these adventurers and native Americans that they attracted, some of the West's major rivers got their names:

Bitterroot. Lewis and Clark, on their 1805 journey, crossed a hazardous mountain range that they called "bitterroot" after a plant—*Lewisia rediviva*—they found growing there. The name "bitterroot" was also applied to a nearby river.

Colorado. Spanish explorers named the river Rio Colorado ("colored river") in 1604 when they came upon it at flood tide and its silt-laden waters were stained a chocolate brown.

Columbia. In 1792, Captain Robert Gray, while on a mission for sea otter, sailed the *Columbia Rediviva* from Boston around the Horn to the mouth of a great river on the Pacific Northwest coast. The captain named the river after his ship.

Deschutes. French fur trappers saw the Deschutes River where it poured into the Columbia River at Celilo Falls. Looking at this breathtaking sight, they labeled the river "Riviere des Chutes," "Riviere aux Chutes," or, "river of falls."

Eel. Dr. Josiah Gregg, a Missouri physician and leader of a party exploring the West, named the river in 1849 after he saw local Indians carrying eel just caught in the water.

Feather. In 1817, Captain Luis Arguello named the river "El Rio de las Plumas," or "River of the Feathers," because of all the waterfowl feathers floating on the water's surface. The "feathers" were probably pollen that had dropped from willows along the river banks.

Gila. Yuma Indians called the river hah-quah-sa-eel ("running salt water") and accented the last syllable. The Spanish shortened the word to the last syllable. Somehow an "a" sound was attached to the name, as was the opening "G."

Humboldt. Persistent pathfinder, John C. Fremont came upon many a river and liked to name them in honor of people. He called this one after Baron Alexander von Humboldt, an explorer and scientist.

John Day. John Day, a young man from Virginia who came West in 1811 with an Astoria-bound party, met an unfortunate death. Suffering from hunger and illness, he was beaten by Indians and left to die along the river that bears his name.

Merced. After a hot and dusty 40-mile march in 1808, Lieutenant Gabriel Moraga and his men came upon a river—a most welcome sight. Deeply grateful, they named it El Rio Nuestra Señora de la Merced, or "the River of Our Lady of Mercy."

Owens. John C. Fremont called the river running along the eastern slope of the Sierra "Owens," after Richard Owens, an Ohioan and a member of his third expedition.

Pend Oreille. French fur trappers named one tribe of Indians living in northern Idaho "Pend Oreille" because of the pendant or shell ornaments hanging in their ear lobes. From this, the lake and the river took its name.

Sacramento. Gabriel Moraga named the upper Sacramento the Feather River in 1808. At the same time, the lower Sacramento was called Rio de San Francisco. Although Moraga's choice was the river's name for awhile, the name Rio del Sacramento soon entered the picture. By the late 1830s, Sacramento River appeared on the maps. Sacramento is Spanish for "holy sacrament."

Salt. The Salt takes its name from the salt beds found along the river in the area of the Salt River Canyon. Until the 1940s the beds were a source of salt for local Indians.

San Joaquin. On his way to Point Reyes, Father Crespi sighted the river in 1772 and called it San Francisco in honor of Saint Francis of Assisi. When Gabriel Moraga came upon the upper stretch of river in 1805, he named it San Joaquin in honor of Saint Joachim.

Smith. Many rivers were named for Jedediah Smith, one of the West's great explorers, but this river in Northern California is the only one that bears his name today. Smith came upon the river in 1828.

Snake. Through a misunderstanding of Indian sign language, the Snake River received its name. Shoshone Indians who occupied the Snake River Plain identified themselves by placing their right hand at waist level, palm facing inward, and then moving their hand in a forward motion, like a fish swimming upstream. They were probably identifying themselves as the people who lived along the river which contained big fish runs. But since the gesture for rattlesnakes was very similar, and because rattlesnakes lived in the countryside, white men called the river Snake.

Truckee. A Paiute Indian named Truckee guided some Missouri pioneers from Battle Mountain, Nevada, to Sutter's Fort. The leader of the party named a river they saw after their able guide.

Tuolumne. Although this name is Indian in origin, its exact meaning is unknown. The most popular version is that it came from the word Talmalamne, meaning "cluster of stone wigwams," since Indians in the area once lived in caves or recesses in the rocks.

Willamette. Although Willamette appears to be a French word, it is actually an anglicized Indian name. No one knows exactly where the name comes from or what it means. One theory is that it was a name of a place along the west bank of the river near present-day Oregon City. The earliest reference to the name is 1811.

IDAHO POWER COMPANY

The Snake gets a big lift. *Electric pumps* **(left),** *developed by private enterprise assisted by Idaho Power Company, have put over 1,000,000 acres of former sagebrush land in the Snake River Valley under cultivation. With electric pumps, the water can be lifted more than 600 feet from the river to the dry but fertile plateaus where a network of canals and pipe carry the water to the crops. One of the projects, the Cottonwood Mutual Canal Company* **(below),** *near Glenns Ferry, boosts the Snake twice. One pumping plant sits at river level, another about halfway up. Electric pumps also tap wells.*

IDAHO POWER COMPANY

Return of lost rivers. *Gushing out of a crumbling basalt wall and into the Snake River are a series of streams seemingly emerging without obvious reason. Past volcanic activity repeatedly pushed the Snake River to the south, filling earlier channels with porous lava. The former river beds have become both reservoirs and conduits, gathering water from areas far to the northeast and carrying it back to the Snake River, where it bursts from the canyon walls in the Hagerman Valley, just west of Buhl, Idaho. Thousand Springs is also believed to be the re-emerging point of the Lost River, so-called because the river is "lost" in a series of lava depressions or sinks.*

FRANK JENSEN

Birds of prey have a protected home in the Snake River Canyon **(below)** south of Boise. Predator birds, such as the golden eagle **(left),** probably are attracted to the canyon because of the healthy population of Townsend ground squirrels that they like to eat, the treeless terrain which allows them an unobstructed view, and the rocky walls in which they like to nest.

The Snake River
Hells Canyon
Deepest of all our gorges

Although most people assume that the Grand Canyon of the Colorado is the deepest gorge on the North American continent, Hells Canyon has it beat by 1,500 feet. This 35-mile section of the Snake, sitting about 5,500 feet beneath the jagged peaks of the Seven Devils Mountains, begins below Hells Canyon Dam. You can tackle the Hells Canyon Seven Devils Scenic Area several ways—by jet boating up river, floating downstream, or hiking the wilderness trails. Although damming has reduced the force of the Snake, Hells Canyon does have its rough moments. But the canyon's real charm lies in the varied and captivating scenery of the surrounding countryside.

FRANK JENSEN

Only way through Hells Canyon is by boat. Boating dates back to the 1860s when The Shoshone, a sternwheeler, carried men and supplies up and down the river between Fort Boise and Hells Canyon. In 1895, another sternwheeler steamed through, and in 1928, Amos Burg, in his "Song of the Winds," made a successful run of the river. Today, there are two ways to boat the Snake. Jet boats (above) leave from Lewiston for short up-river trips. Floating, increasing in popularity each year, begins just below Hells Canyon Dam and ends six days and 85 miles later at the Snake's confluence with the Grande Ronde, 30 miles south of Lewiston. The most exciting white water and the craggiest landscape are between the dam and Sheep Creek. Then the water calms down and the rugged basaltic rock formations give way to rolling grassy hillsides.

Hauntingly beautiful country borders the Hells Canyon area of the Snake River. The region is roadless, but trails cross the rugged, moody, and almost lunar-type landscape. Hikers *(above)* rest on a grassy knoll and relax to the sound of a flute. A pack train *(left)* slices across rolling hillsides for a wilderness adventure in the 130,000-acre Hells Canyon-Seven Devils Scenic Area.

Columbia River Basin　97

Across the Idaho Wilderness
Legendary River of No Return

The Salmon's "nickname" dates back to 1805, when Captain William Clark scouted the river as a possible route west across Idaho. The precipitous canyon walls caused Clark great concern—if the water proved too rough, there could be no turning back. Charging through the second deepest canyon on the North American Continent, the Salmon River remains as primitive today as it was during explorer days. A rugged road follows the north side from Salmon, Idaho as far west as Corn Creek; for the next 79 miles, the only way out is to ride the river. The Salmon's Middle Fork also churns through untouched wilderness, its natural state preserved by the Wild and Scenic Rivers Act.

LINDA COHEN

At the point of no return. Corn Creek, 79 miles west of Salmon, Idaho, is the last chance to turn back. If you choose to float on downstream, you have a six-day commitment to the Salmon River.

Playful river characters. Having an oily waterproof fur coat, webbed toes, sleek tails, and a great love of the water, otters are beautifully adapted to river life. Although otters frequent streams in forested areas, they shun man and are scarcely ever seen. At home on land as well as on water, they like to scamper across rocks or bask lazily in the sun.

"Down in the depths, miles from nowhere" aptly describes the feeling when floating the main or the Middle Fork of the Salmon. These rivers flow through very primitive areas in central Idaho, with no roads or signs of civilization for hundreds of miles. The Middle Fork is noted for its intense and frequent white water. The main Salmon is one of the better swimming rivers—its cool waters are the only way to beat the canyon's confining heat.

Experiencing a River...there are many ways

The method you choose for riding a river depends on the river and you. Innertubes require calm water, whereas rubber rafts (available in a variety of sizes) can glide through quiet stretches or tackle white water. Wooden dories, good for drift fishing, are easy to maneuver because of their build—wide amidship and pointed or narrow at both ends. Kayaks, fairly lightweight and made of fiberglass, swiftly skim the surface of the water. Kayaks may not sink, but they can overturn. Sportyaks, fairly recent additions to the river run scene, are 7-foot polyethylene skiffs designed with the novice rower in mind.

ELIZABETH JOY

JACK McDOWELL

Rubber rafts can be used on both fast and slow water. Basic innertube (above right) is great for relaxing on calm stretches, whereas a two-man raft (right) can negotiate small patches of fast water. For the rough water, large pontoon-type rafts (above) are best.

JACK McDOWELL

If you have the muscle, try an oar-powered sport boat. Kayaker *(top right)* negotiates current and maintains balance by manipulating paddle. Sportyak *(top left)* and dory *(middle)* are stable crafts because of their size and shape. But the power boat *(left)* is by far the best way to get upstream.

Columbia River Basin   101

More Rivers in the Columbia Basin

Palouse River. Moving across southeastern Washington's rolling plateau country is the Palouse. About 40 miles before emptying into the Snake River, it cuts a deep, terraced canyon and takes a spectacular 185-foot plunge. Palouse Falls is within Palouse Falls State Park.

WILLIAM A. PEDERSEN

S.C. WILSON

HUGH PARADISE

Kootenai River. Although the Kootenai River spends time in northwest Montana and northeast Idaho, half of its 448 miles lies in Canada. Benchlands border most of the river, but occasionally it takes a plunge.

Bruneau River. A tributary to the Snake River, the Bruneau slices through southwestern Idaho's sagebrush and sand country. A good glimpse of the river and the surrounding terrain comes at the Bruneau Canyon Overlook, where the river flows 800 feet beneath you.

Owyhee River. A recent addition to the river-running scene, the Owyhee can be navigated only in spring after snow melt swells the river and cushions the rapids. A tributary to the Snake, the Owyhee journeys north through the hot and barren southeastern Oregon desert. Two stretches of the Owyhee are designated by the state of Oregon as natural river areas.

Clearwater River. A highway for Lewis and Clark in 1805, the Clearwater for most of its path lies in northern Idaho's primitive wilderness. The Middle Fork of the river from Kooskia to its headwaters is part of the Federal Wild and Scenic Rivers Act of 1968. After the damming of the North Fork with Dworshak *(below)*, log tows ceased on the river.

Okanogan River. Coming from Canada (where it is spelled Okanagan), the Okanogan proceeds south through eastern Washington's apple valleys before meeting the Columbia. The Okanogan River is part of the Omak Stampede. Dare-devil riders charge down a steep hill and across the river in a wild, dusty, wet race.

Columbia River Basin   103

THE COLORADO
Precious Water for

DAVID MUENCH

RIVER BASIN the Arid Southwest

Grand Falls of the Little Colorado during spring runoff

If you look at a map of the Colorado River Basin, you'll notice two striking features. First, the map looks lopsided, for all of the water comes from the Rocky Mountains. Second, few rivers make up this important system.

The main river within the basin—the Colorado—originates in western Colorado and passes through six states before meeting the Gulf of California. Tributaries are the Green, Gunnison, San Juan, Little Colorado, and Gila rivers. The total area within the Colorado River Basin is 243,000 square miles. This is a land of few cities; the largest in the Colorado Basin is Phoenix.

Because the paths of the rivers are through semi-arid to arid country, their flows are definitely seasonal. Fed by mountain snow melt, they burst forth with water in spring, then dwindle sharply as summer fades into fall. If life is to be sustained in the arid southwest, river water needs to be saved for use year round. Storage dams on tributaries as well as on the main stem conserve spring runoff. Seven states—all of which have water rights to the Colorado—have an agreement as to how much water each gets annually. Damming has also reduced the amount of silt carried by the Colorado.

The most outstanding and most prevalent physical feature of the Colorado River Basin is the sedimentary rock strata, uplifted thousands of feet, faulted, and eroded into broad plateaus, mesas, buttes, natural bridges, and deep canyons.

(For a map of the Colorado River Basin and its relation to the rest of the West, turn to either the inside front or back cover.)

THE COLORADO RIVER
Highly Respected, Greatly Overworked

Longest river in the West, running from the Rockies to the Gulf of California, the Colorado—largely tamed by man—still boasts some grand canyons

A different river in its beginning than in its ending, the Colorado surges fast and full from Rocky Mountain snow melt. By the time it reaches the Gulf of California—1,450 miles later—the Colorado is just a trickle.

Where does all the water go? First of all, the river, flowing through arid country, is not replenished with water by spring, summer, and fall rains. Secondly, the Colorado must keep seven states in water. Each of the seven, by agreement, receives an annual allotment of water from the river and its main tributaries. Hoover and Glen Canyon dams are the key storage facilities, holding back spring runoff so water can be released for downstream irrigation throughout the year.

Hydroelectric power, not an initial reason for the damming, has been an important by-product. Another benefit is the recreational reservoirs. Lakes Powell, Mead, Mojave, and Havasu provide acres and acres of water for fishing, boating, and swimming in a hot and dry desert. Reservoirs also trap sediment, greatly reducing the amount of silt carried by the Colorado.

But for all its accomplishments, the Colorado is probably best known for the masterpiece it carved—the Grand Canyon. Contained within a national monument and a national park, the Grand Canyon can be viewed from above. But a float trip through the depths of the canyon brings you in close contact with the powerful action of the river.

Although the Colorado is one of the West's most important rivers, no metropolitan area sits along its banks. Access roads are few; nine-tenths of the Colorado is cliffbound, and 1,000 of its miles run through deep canyons.

RON COHEN

Best river to run in the West. *A 9 to 12-day ride through the Grand Canyon takes you through rapids at their wildest. But the white water is not the canyon's only attraction. In the canyon walls stands the geological history of the earth. Indian ruins are testimonials to the canyon's prehistoric inhabitants. And surprises—from side glens and waterfalls to bighorn sheep—can be around the next bend.*

Like giant sentries, intriguing rock formations are ever present in western Colorado. Rather than hug the river, they stand back, allowing the Colorado to pass through a fairly wide valley.

ED COOPER

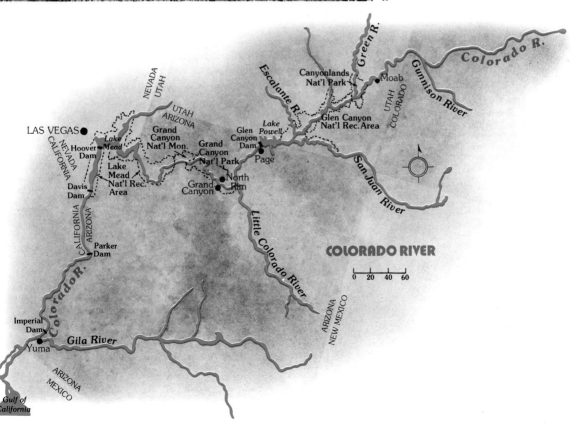

Colorado R.

Green R.

Escalante R.

Canyonlands Nat'l Park

Moab

Gunnison River

UTAH
COLORADO

NEVADA
UTAH

UTAH
ARIZONA

Glen Canyon Nat'l Rec. Area

Lake Powell

LAS VEGAS

Hoover Dam

Lake Mead

Grand Canyon Nat'l Mon.

Glen Canyon Dam

NEVADA
CALIFORNIA

Lake Mead Nat'l Rec. Area

Grand Canyon Nat'l Park

Page

San Juan River

Davis Dam

Grand Canyon

North Rim

CALIFORNIA
ARIZONA

Parker Dam

Little Colorado River

COLORADO RIVER

0 20 40 60

Colorado R.

Imperial Dam

Yuma

Gila River

ARIZONA
NEW MEXICO

ARIZONA
MEXICO

Gulf of California

Colorado River Basin   107

The Canyons of the Colorado
Terra Incognito on the map until 1869

Since 400 A.D. various groups of Indians have lived in the canyons of the Colorado. White man first sighted the awesome spectacle sometime around 1540. But the Grand Canyon of the Colorado was not officially mapped until Civil War veteran Major John Wesley Powell took his historic adventure into the great unknown. His mission was to travel the Green River to where it meets the Grand River (today's upper Colorado) and then follow the Colorado to its confluence with the Virgin River. He began his journey on May 24, 1869, with ten men and four boats. Thirteen weeks later with six men and two boats, he emerged from the canyon.

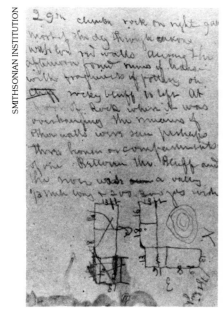

"Steady . . . hard on the left"—
those were the kinds of orders Major Powell shouted to his men as the wooden boats were tossed about in the wild rapids of the Colorado. During Powell's two voyages down the Colorado, he kept a daily journal on long, narrow strips of brown paper, recording impressions and facts of the canyons. Portions of his journal appeared in Scribner's magazine in 1874 and 1875, accompanied by sketches made by Powell's contemporaries.

Businesslike approach to running a river. When Major Powell set off on his second trip down the Green and the Colorado rivers in 1871, he had a photographer on hand to snap the historic moment.

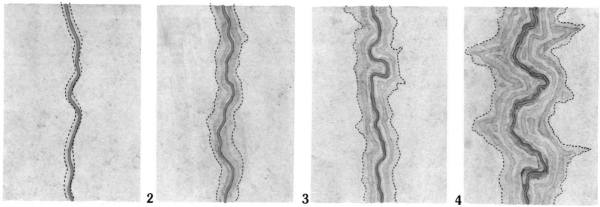

1   2   3   4

How the Colorado cut the Grand Canyon. 1) A lazy river meandered through a gently sloping plain, cutting a shallow channel into the earth. 2) Pressure within the earth slowly tilted the surface, causing the river to run faster and cut deeper. Land on both sides gradually eroded into the river, and the canyon took on a V shape. 3) Sides of the V-shaped canyon began to break down as forces of erosion attacked them. 4) Over the ages the river continued to cut deeper, following its original configuration. As the river cut, the break-up of the canyon walls became accelerated, opening an ever-widening gap.

Dammed to Tame the Unruly Waters

Hoover was the first...but not the last

It may be difficult today to picture the Colorado River before 1931, when its rampaging waters ran wildly through steep, rocky canyons. But a visit to Hoover Dam and Lake Mead gives an excellent idea of the monumental structure it took to contain the powerful flow and the amount of water saved that used to run out to sea. Hoover and Glen Canyon dams, completed in 1935 and 1964 respectively, are the two keys to controlling the river. Additional regulations are imposed by three major units and about a dozen minor ones on Colorado tributaries.

Black Canyon —before, during, and after construction of Hoover Dam. Original dam site was Boulder Canyon, but the hard and solid bedrock walls of Black Canyon, a few miles downstream, won out. Work began in 1931 on a concrete arch-gravity structure. Because of the tremendous amount of concrete to be poured (3¼ million cubic yards), the dam was built in blocks **(top right)**. Within each block ran steel tubing carrying cold water to control and hasten the cooling of the concrete. (If the concrete had been poured in a single solid mass, it would have taken more than 100 years to dry!) Straddling the Arizona/Nevada border, the 721-foot-high dam was completed in the record time of five years.

BUREAU OF RECLAMATION

BUREAU OF RECLAMATION

BUREAU OF RECLAMATION

THE COLORADO...
SLAVE TO SEVEN STATES

At the beginning of the 20th century, the lower California desert was being promoted as an imperial valley—one ideally suited to farming, with a 365-day-a-year growing season and plenty of water from the nearby mighty Colorado River. But the Colorado was not only mighty—it was also unpredictable. Floods could do as much damage as drought. If a dam could be built to store the heavy spring runoff, water could be controlled to prevent floods and to be available for year-round irrigation.

The people of the Imperial Valley, interested in protecting their investment, turned to the federal government for help. Studies and more studies were undertaken. The problems involved more than just determining the best site for a dam. Seven states had claim to the river, and a major question was how to allocate the water.

Colorado River Compact. In 1922 each of the seven states (California, Arizona, Nevada, New Mexico, Colorado, Utah, Wyoming) sent a representative to Washington, D.C. Under the direction of then Secretary of Commerce Herbert Hoover, the group devised the Colorado River Compact. Essentially, the Compact divided the Colorado River Basin into approximately equal-sized upper and lower basins and gave each exclusive use of 7,500,000 acre-feet of water per annum. If more water were available, the Lower Basin could receive an additional 1,000,000 acre-feet per annum. Actual division of water among individual states was to be determined later. The dividing point was to be Lees Ferry.

Boulder Canyon Project Act. In 1928 Congress approved the Colorado River Compact and authorized the Department of Interior through its Bureau of Reclamation to construct a major storage dam at either Black or Boulder canyons and a canal system connecting the Imperial and Coachella valleys with the Colorado.

The storage dam, known today as Hoover Dam, would be built in Black Canyon for flood control, regulation of the flow, storage and delivery of stored water for reclamation of public lands, generation of electricity, and sediment control. Backup reservoir Lake Mead could hold more than twice the river's annual runoff at this point.

The All-American and Coachella canals would receive water through Imperial Dam to irrigate close to 700,000 acres of land in the Imperial Valley in southeastern California.

Colorado River Storage Project. In 1948 the Upper Basin States agreed on how to divide their share of river water. Of the 7,500,000 acre-feet per annum, Arizona was entitled to 50,000 acre-feet per annum; of the remainder, 51¾ per cent was allocated to Colorado, 11¼ per cent to New Mexico, 23 per cent to Utah, and 14 per cent to Wyoming. Numerous conflicts kept the Lower Basin States from agreement. In 1963 a Supreme Court ruling entitled California to 4,400,000 acre-feet, Arizona 2,800,000 acre-feet, and Nevada 300,000 acre-feet per annum. If additional water were available, 50 per cent would go to both Arizona and California. Nevada could get 4 per cent from Arizona's share.

The Upper Basin States, concerned about a shortage of water in a low rainfall year, decided to ensure their annual allotment by catching the river's flow above Hoover Dam with storage dams on the Colorado and major tributaries. The key structure is Glen Canyon Dam, completed in 1964, and its reservoir Lake Powell.

Three other Bureau of Reclamation dams contribute strongly to the Project: Flaming Gorge on the Green River in the northeast corner of Utah, Blue Mesa and Morrow Point on the Gunnison River in Colorado, and Navajo on the San Juan River in northern New Mexico.

Other Controls. Besides the major storage dams, other projects make demands on the river. The Colorado River Aqueduct, built by the Metropolitan Water District of Southern California, pipes river water west to 122 municipalities in the Los Angeles area for domestic purposes. Controlling factor for the 242-mile-long aqueduct is Parker Dam. Davis Dam's primary responsibility is to ensure Mexico 1,500,000 acre-feet annually.

Future Plans. In the early 1980s, the Colorado River will journey east to central Arizona to supplement the flows of the Gila and Salt rivers and relieve the heavy tapping of the ground water. Beginning point of the Central Arizona Project will be at Lake Havasu, behind Parker Dam.

Looking high as well as forward, the Colorado River Basin Pilot Project is experimenting with cloud seeding in Colorado's San Juan Mountains. Cloud seeding could increase the snowfall in the mountains 10 to 30 per cent.

Colorado River Basin Storage Projects. Dotted line is the division between Upper Basin and Lower Basin states.

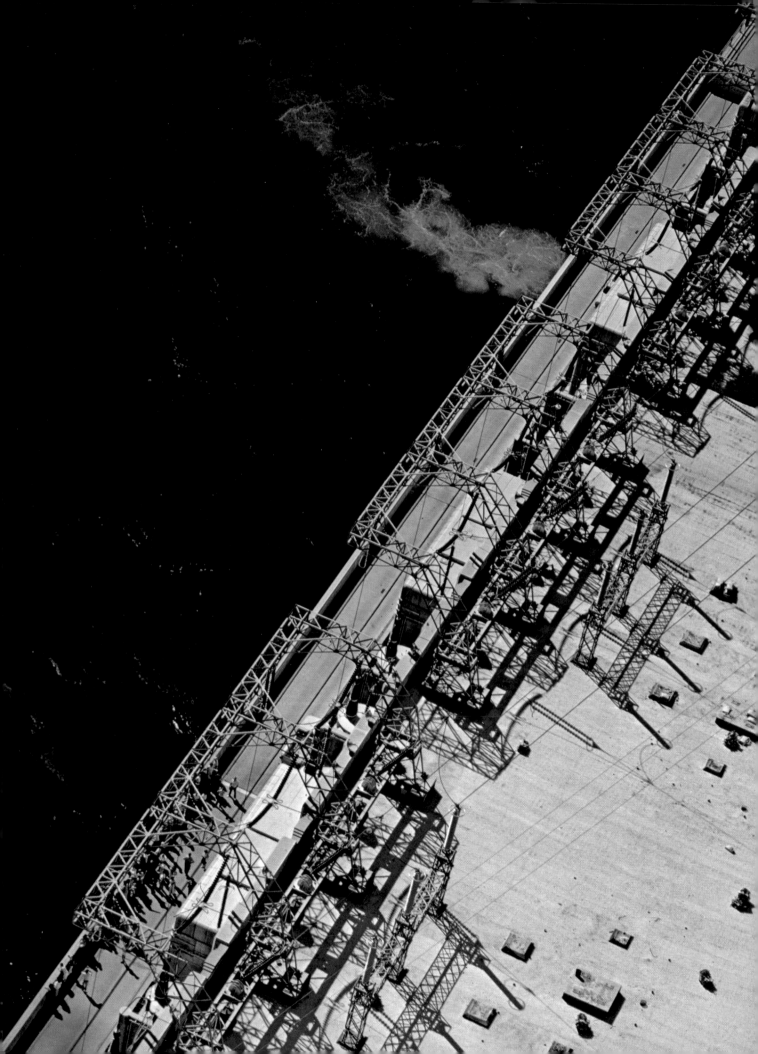

JACK McDOWELL

Electricity for three states.
Hydroelectric power created at Hoover Dam (total rated capacity—1,344,800 kilowatts) is transmitted via power lines from the dam to its final destination. Principal contractors for this energy are the states of Arizona and Nevada, the City of Los Angeles Department of Water and Power, the Southern California Edison Company, the Metropolitan Water District of Southern California, and the cities of Glendale, Burbank, and Pasadena.

Powerhouse spews water *(near top of photo) into the canyon-darkened Colorado. The water released from the power plant at Hoover Dam has just turned one of the 17 turbines—the number used depends on the amount of water required downstream. (Water cannot be released through Hoover Dam without generating electricity.) This view of the power plant is from the top of the dam, looking straight down the face.*

The Colorado River
The last of the Colorado
One last watering stop before crossing the border

When the Colorado River reaches Imperial Dam, 303 miles below Hoover Dam and 18 miles northeast of Yuma, Arizona, it is just a fraction of its original size. And of the water reaching Imperial Dam, four-fifths is diverted from the river into the All-American Canal System to irrigate thousands of acres of farmland in the Imperial and Coachella valleys and those lands under the Yuma Project. What's left of the river—only a trickle and full of salt— moves across the border into Mexico on its way to the sea.

JACK McDOWELL

Water at work in the southeastern California desert. The All-American Canal System irrigates 530,000 acres in the Imperial Valley via the 80-mile-long All-American Canal (completed in 1940) and 78,000 acres in the Coachella Valley via the 123-mile-long Coachella Canal (completed in 1950). Main crops in the Imperial Valley are alfalfa hay and seed, cotton, sugar beets, winter vegetables, barley, flax, cantaloupes, and sorghum. Although the Coachella Valley produces about 90 per cent of the nation's dates, the biggest money crop is table grapes. Intake for the canal system is Imperial Dam.

JACK McDOWELL

JACK McDOWELL

June in January. *Winter months are busy months in the fields in the Imperial and Coachella valleys. Lettuce **(above)**, biggest crop in the Imperial Valley, and carrots **(left)** are harvested by hand in late December and early January.*

...LAST OF THE COLORADO

JACK McDOWELL

Headed for Mexico. The Colorado is not much of a river as it crosses the border into Mexico and is diverted through Morelos Dam and into the Mexicali Valley. The heavy concentration of saline in the water poses great difficulties to the Mexicali cotton crop.

JACK McDOWELL

Headed for California. Water is released from Imperial Dam, then routed through desilting basins before entering the All-American Canal System. Salt content of the river still remains somewhat of a problem, although Imperial Valley farmers have installed miles of underground drainage gutters to catch the saline water that accumulates in the soil.

Colorado River Basin   117

The Colorado River
The Grand Canyon
Truly, the grandest canyon of all

A million things wrapped up into one package—that is the Colorado River through its Grand Canyon. It is white frothy rapids; it is water crystal clear and smooth-as-glass. It is water of many colors—emerald green, sky blue, brown, aquamarine, sometimes black. For centuries the river has ground its way through the rock, cutting truly indescribable canyons and exposing the history of the earth. It has been said before, and it will be said again: the only way to believe the Grand Canyon is to see it. And the only way to see it for its entire length is a 9 to 12-day river trip covering the 300-mile stretch from Lees Ferry to South Cove (Lake Mead).

RON COHEN

Taking the plunge. *Roaring water signals white water ahead, and suddenly the "hole" sucks in the raft. You bounce up and down with the violent thrashing of the water until you're through the rapid—wet, excited, and anxious for more. Throughout the 280-mile Grand Canyon run, more than 200 rapids—some big, some not so big—make for a thrilling ride. The most intense rapid is Lava Falls, often rated 10 on a 0 to 10 scale (10 being the most difficult). Lava Falls, sometimes referred to as Vulcan Rapid, was created a million years ago when an immense lava flow blocked the river. The Colorado slowly ground away at the damming lava, freeing itself but leaving boulders exposed.*

 RON COHEN

No place for acrophobes. *Rafts pull over to shore in Marble Canyon, and river runners make the steep hike up to Nankoweap ruins. Sitting one thousand feet above the Colorado River, the Indian ruins, just one of over 500 sites found within Grand Canyon National Park, consist of about a half-dozen rooms, each 6 feet long, 4 feet high, and 3 feet deep. These may have been for storing food grown along Nankoweap Creek.*

RON COHEN

Colorado River Basin   119

The Colorado River
...GRAND CANYON

Near Cardenas Creek at Hilltop Indian Ruins, the Colorado twists *smoothly around the canyon walls. In the normal light of day, the water shines deep blue, and the walls display their subtle pinks and browns.*

RON COHEN

Warm waters of the Little Colorado are colored aquamarine by mineral salts. A delightful Hopi legend has the Indians' ancestors emerging from the underworld through a spring in a travertine dome, situated on the Little Colorado just 5 miles east of the Grand Canyon.

Havasu Falls may look as if it belongs in the South Seas, but it plunges over travertine ledges into Havasu Creek. You can reach Havasu two ways—by running the Colorado or by following a foot and mule trail between the rim and tiny Havasupai Indian Reservation.

Colorado River Basin   121

The Colorado River
...GRAND CANYON

RON COHEN

Passing the time of day *on a sandy beach along the Colorado are wild burros, descendants from forebears brought into the canyon by prospectors. The shy creatures are usually sighted along the lower section of the Grand Canyon run.*

Bighorn sheep *live in the lower elevations of the Grand Canyon. Rare specimens, occasionally they show themselves, but the eye has to be sharp, for these desert animals blend in almost too perfectly with the rocky canyon walls. Bighorn sheep do not shed their horns. The horns continue to grow and curl as the sheep ages. Horns on young lamb have not yet sprouted.*

History of the earth. *Sculptured canyon walls—in some places very vertical and in others more open—border the entire run of the Grand Canyon. In the rocks of the wall, tidily deposited layers of lava tell the story of the earth. Oldest rock in the canyon dates back two billion years; youngest rocks are only 235 million years old.*

Colorado River Basin   123

The Colorado River

The Gentle Colorado

Either a slow current...or no current

Lakes Powell, Mead, Mojave, and Havasu may have inundated many a rapid, but they provide miles and miles of flat water for desert boating, fishing, and swimming enthusiasts. Crystal clear and unbelievably blue, the lakes stretch endlessly in rugged mountainous terrain or in sandstone country. Below Havasu, the lowest storage reservoir, the Colorado becomes a river again, with the return of its current (although upstream controls keep it slow) and riverbank vegetation.

JACK McDOWELL

Exiting from Cascade Canyon, power boat heads for another of Lake Powell's almost 100 side canyons. The fiordlike inlets are twisting and very narrow, often shadowed by steep vertical walls or overhanging cliffs. Contrasting sharply with the reddish sandstone canyon walls is the lake's extremely blue and mirrorlike surface. The reservoir behind Glen Canyon Dam, Lake Powell has a 160-mile shoreline. For the taking in the lake's water are trout, largemouth bass, and kokanee salmon.

Lake Mead, the reservoir behind Hoover Dam, provides a 250-square-mile water playground for desert boaters, water-skiers, and swimmers. When the water level is up, power boats can travel up Lake Mead as far as the southern entrance to the Grand Canyon—a good day's trip. The white band around the base of the mountains marks high water.

Colorado River Basin 125

The Colorado River
...GENTLE COLORADO

Silent canoes, silent country. This is Picacho area with Chocolate Mountains in background. A good time to canoe the lower Colorado is during the winter, for the desert sun is seasonally benign, bass and catfish are plentiful, mosquitoes are mercifully scarce, and the river's controlled water level is down—lessening power boat traffic. Two stretches of the lower river offer the canoeist a taste of desert river wilderness. One, below Needles, takes one day; the other, below Blythe, takes two or three days with camping beside the river.

DARROW M. WATT

WHEN A RIVER CREATED A SEA

"Stop it at all costs" were the orders of E. H. Harriman, president of Southern Pacific, to his engineers in the battle to stop the rampaging Colorado in the early 1900s. And stop it they did—two years and 3 million dollars later.

In prehistoric times the Colorado was an unpredictable, raging, silt-laden river. In fact, it carried so much silt that a natural levee (10 miles wide by 30 miles long) formed at the river's mouth, dividing the Gulf of California in half. The Colorado flowed on the southeastern side of the levee, creating a salt water lake on the upper side of the gulf. Gradually the lake evaporated, leaving a 2,100-square-mile arid basin, later to be known as the Salton Sink. Several hundred years later the Colorado abandoned the gulf and poured into the

February, 1905, the Colorado switched its path at the delta and surged with strength through the opened irrigation canals.

The California Development Company turned to the Southern Pacific for help in saving the Imperial Valley. Harriman rounded up funds, engineers, and workers to concentrate on channeling the river back to its original path. First attempts were with sandbag and pile dams; these the Colorado just carried away. Dumping rock and earth into the chocolate-brown waters was more successful—at least on the sixth attempt. The river reverted back to its proper path on November 4, 1906, after rail cars had poured tons of fill into the angry waters.

But the Colorado wasn't going to behave for long. A month later it broke loose again and headed for the Imperial Valley, surging down the valley sides to the bottom to form the Salton Sea. Encouraged by the government, Southern Pacific continued to fight the battle with the stubborn and powerful river. The new plan called for construct-

SOUTHERN PACIFIC

dry Salton Sink, creating a fresh water lake. Centuries later, the Colorado turned back to the gulf, leaving the Sink to dry in the hot sun.

In the late 1800s, developers saw great agricultural potential in the Salton Sink if enough Colorado River water could be carried to the silt-rich soil. The California Development Company built canals from the river to the ancient lake bed and, for promotional reasons, changed the name from Salton Sink to Imperial Valley. Settlers moved in and grew barley, alfalfa, cotton, grapes, melons, oranges, vegetables, lemons, and other crops.

But trouble was coming from the Colorado. In 1904 the irrigation canals became clogged with silt. Developers thought that, if they widened the canals, the extra flow would carry the silt away. In

ing two railroad trestles over the gap (1,100 feet wide and 40 feet deep) and dumping fill from 1,000 flat cars and side dump cars onto the trestles into the water faster than it could be carried away or swallowed by the silt. Three times the river conquered the trestles, but finally the first trestle was completed. For 15 consecutive days, rock and earth were dumped into the Colorado. On February 10, 1907, the crevasse was closed and the river returned to its original channel, saving the Imperial Valley.

Evidence of this wild rampage exists today in the Salton Sea (part of which is a national recreation area), whose water surface stands at 234 feet below sea level, only 46 feet higher than the lowest point in Death Valley.

THE GREEN RIVER
Shades of the Colorado

Flowing almost directly south, the Green crosses tranquil valleys before plunging through eastern Utah's deep and intricately carved canyonlands

At one time the Green River was considered the Colorado, but today its delegated status is that of a main tributary. Traveling south for 730 miles from the Continental Divide to its merger with the Colorado River in Canyonlands National Park, the Green River carves a path and shows a personality similar to that of the main stem.

The Green River begins in western Wyoming, meandering through pleasant valleys and highlands. After entering Utah, it undergoes a definite change of character, slicing through deep canyons bordered by rocky plateaus in desolate, almost inaccessible country.

In the rugged areas, the Green River can be reached in Flaming Gorge National Recreation Area and Dinosaur National Monument. A road meets the Green at Ouray and Green River, Utah. The rest of the river is roadless covered only through a float trip.

The first inhabitants of the area were Indians, who left petroglyphs on cliff walls. In 1824 the mountain men and William Ashley arrived and chose to tackle the Green (near present-day Jensen, Utah) in boats of buffalo hides. The total isolation of the Green made the area a retreat for outlaws.

John Wesley Powell really put the Green on the map. His journey through the Grand Canyon began on the Green.

So much of the Green remains a wilderness river, making its personality similar to pioneer days. But two dams—Fontenelle and Flaming Gorge—on the upper Green control the water for irrigation as part of the Colorado River Basin Storage Project (see page 111).

FRANK JENSEN

Erosive action of the Green shows sharply as the river makes a turn around Steamboat Rock in Dinosaur National Monument. Although a few back-country roads travel within the monument, floating the river provides the closest look at its power. Of special interest within the monument is the Dinosaur Quarry. Excavated river sediment dating back 140 million years reveals that 14 species of dinosaurs once claimed the territory.

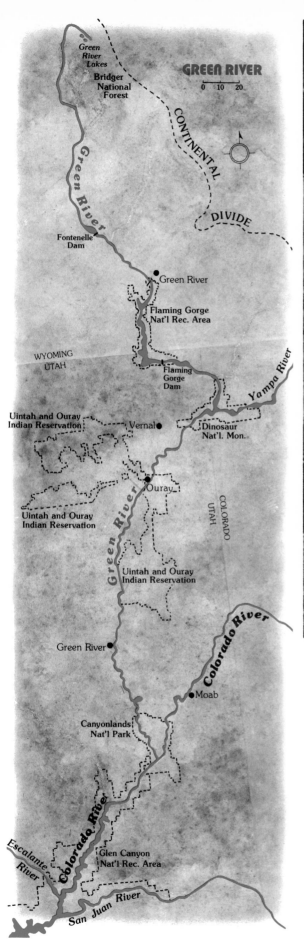

RON COHEN

Islands of rocks. *Wherever you are on the Green in Utah's canyon country, the river is bordered by plateaus and unusual rock formations. Occasionally, it's dotted with free-standing rocks.*

Colorado River Basin 129

The Green River
Canyon Country
Effortless drifting through an eroded desert

The Green River from Ouray, Utah, to its confluence with the Colorado River in Canyonlands National Park passes through a land of unusual sandstone formations carved by the winds of time. In the desolate canyons surrounding the river, prehistoric Indians, fur trappers, and the illustrious Butch Cassidy once roamed. Since the region is remote, the only way to see the Green is to float it. Trips from Ouray travel through the Green River Wilderness; those that begin at Green River, Utah, pass through the uniquely and intricately carved canyonlands of eastern Utah.

Rocky mesas and plateaus border the Green River as it journeys south through eastern Utah on its way to the Colorado River. Until the Green meets the Colorado in a "y" in Canyonlands National Park *(above)*, the water is relatively calm, making for a leisurely float trip. Note the color of the Colorado, remarkably darker than that of the Green.

Doll House (just one of mar intriguing rock formations), boilir water, and steep canyor characterize Cataract Canyon—th stretch of river just below th confluence of the Green and th Colorado. The only entry in Cataract Canyon is by rafting th Green from Green River, Utah rafting the Colorado from Moa

In Labyrinth Canyon the Green River makes little progress as it twists
and turns for 7 miles. The long, spectacular meander ends at Bowknot
Bend, where floaters can stretch their legs by scrambling across
Bowknot's narrow neck to meet the rafts on the other side. Labyrinth
Canyon is between Green River, Utah, and Canyonlands National Park.

RON COHEN

RON COHEN

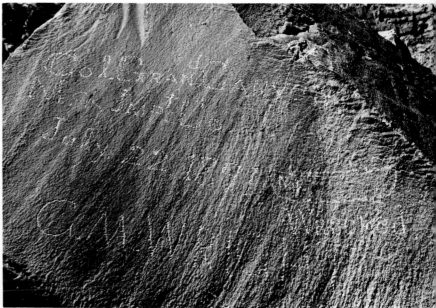

RON COHEN

Adventurers *of bygone days liked to leave evidence of their explorations. One inscription found carved in Hell Roaring Canyon is dated 1836. These three etched in stone at Bowknot Bend indicate that floaters passed this way in 1891, 1905, and 1927.*

River Runners going about their daily routine

The aroma of breakfast filters through camp as a typical day on a river run begins. After a leisurely meal, it's time to roll up sleeping bags, pack gear, and load rafts to continue the journey downstream. Much of the day is spent on the river. Guided by skilled oarsmen, rafts bounce through the fast water and drift through calm stretches. Wild rapids give rafters a soaking, but stops for lunch or a hike provide time to dry off. The more placid sections may call for a spirited waterfight or a refreshing swim. Camp is made before dusk. Dinner is served around a campfire, and as the embers die, so does the day. River runners head for their sleeping bags to spend the night under a star-speckled sky, the river the only noise in the still night.

RON COHEN

Eating: Always hungry and very thirsty, river runners all agree they are well fed. Breakfast (right) is prepared at camp, lunch (above) is served at a sandy beach downstream. Dinner is a campfire occasion.

RON COHEN

Riding the rapids: Smiling faces indicate a successful trip through the white water. How wet you get depends on intensity of rapid, type and size of raft, and your position on the craft.

Free time: During lunch break or after camp has been made, you can hike the nearby countryside, enjoy the refreshing shower of a waterfall (*left*), or simply cool off with a cup of river water (*below*).

Colorado River Basin   135

The Green River
In the Wind River Range
At the top of the Divide...the beginning of the Green

Almost at the peak of the Continental Divide lie the Green River Lakes, birthplace of the Green River. The upper Green, much different in character from the lower Green, moves slowly—but sometime with vigor—through meadows dotted with wildflowers and grazing cattle. The river beckons fishermen and canoers; the surrounding wilderness welcomes the hiker and backpacker. The Wind River Range, as the area is known, is reachable only in summer by an unimproved road north of Cora, Wyoming.

Rough enough to be exciting but not so rough that it will tip you over, the upper Green is just right for kayaking, sportyaking, or canoeing. Shore is never too far away, and the water is not terribly deep. But no matter what kind of boating you decide to do, you must bring your own craft.

Trout abound in this rarely fished spot. Just below Green River Lakes, the Green River meanders through tranquil country where cattle graze and pines stand tall. In the background is Square Top Mountain, an unmistakable landmark on the horizon.

Green River Lakes area is good pack-in country. Trails, varying in lengths and degrees, traverse Bridger National Forest.

Colorado River Basin 137

THE SALT RIVER
Keeping Phoenix Alive

Mountain-born but following a desert path for 200 miles, the Salt vanishes after a stopover in Phoenix

The Salt is not a well-known river. Nor is it a large river in terms of volume or length. But the Salt has an important job to do, and it does it well. It provides precious water for one of the Southwest's major metropolitan areas: Phoenix.

A desert river for most of its path, the Salt originates at the meeting of the Black and the White rivers in eastern Arizona's White Mountains. As the Salt heads west, it cuts an impressive canyon, crossed by a highway, and then loses itself in Roosevelt Lake.

Use of the Salt dates back to prehistoric times, when desert dwellers farmed the river valley and built irrigation canals to water their crops. Around 1400 A.D., these people disappeared. In the 1860s, white men came to the valley and patterned their irrigation system after that of the Indians.

As the population grew, the need for a central control over water rights arose. This led to the Salt River Project, the first multi-purpose reclamation project passed under the Federal Reclamation Act of 1902. A private company, the Salt River Project carefully controls the river and distributes its waters to the people of Phoenix and its suburbs. Four storage dams (with hydroelectric plants) on the Salt, two storage dams on the Verde, and a network (1,300 miles) of canals through the metropolitan area are the backbone of the system.

The Salt is not all business. Localites sail, motor boat, and swim on the reservoirs and lazily float the river between the reservoirs and canals.

For all the work it does for Phoenix, the Salt pays a high price. West of the city, the river bed is dry. The water is all used up.

JACK McDOWELL

Intent on tubing. Phoenix residents flock to the Salt to float and keep cool during summer's sizzling heat. The most popular place to innertube is the stretch just below Stewart Mountain Dam.

Grand Canal, glistening in the light of the setting sun, is just one of a half-dozen canals carrying the Salt's water across Phoenix.

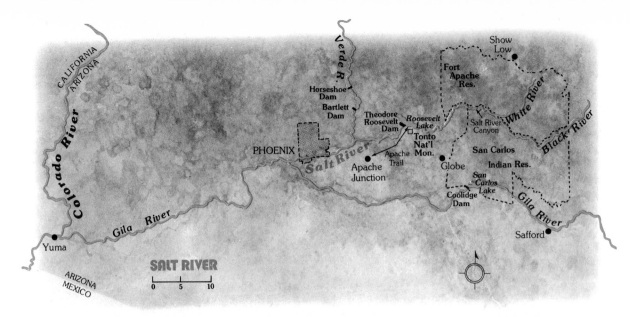

SALT RIVER

CALIFORNIA
ARIZONA

Colorado River

Verde R.

Horseshoe
Dam

Bartlett
Dam

Theodore
Roosevelt
Dam

*Roosevelt
Lake*

Tonto
Nat'l
Mon.

PHOENIX

Salt River

Apache
Junction

Apache
Trail

Show
Low

Fort
Apache
Res.

White River

Salt River
Canyon

Black River

San Carlos

Globe

Indian Res.

*San
Carlos
Lake*

Coolidge
Dam

Gila River

Gila River

Safford

Yuma

Gila River

ARIZONA
MEXICO

SALT RIVER

0   5   10

Early Settlers

Perhaps too much water drove them away

From about 300 B.C. to 1400 A.D., a culture referred to as the River Hohokam inhabited the Gila and Salt river valleys. The people were agricultural, dependent on the natural flooding of the rivers to water their corn, beans, squash, and cotton. Dates vary, but around 700 A.D. they began irrigating crops through an elaborate system of canals. Around 1400 A.D., the river people mysteriously disappeared. Theories point to partial or total destruction of their canals from excessive rainfall and a drop in crop productivity from too much salt in the soil. Others believe drought, enemies, or pestilence may have forced them away.

JACK McDOWELL

Hillside homes for Indian farmers were Gila Cliff Dwelling *(right)* and Tonto National Monument *(below)*. Inhabitants of Gila farmed the mesas and the land along the river. Tonto's residents were Salado Indians who farmed the fertile Salt River plains, and, through an extensive system of canals, irrigated their crops. The irrigation canals were in existence until 1911 when Roosevelt Lake was filled. Canal ruins can still be seen at Pueblo Grande in Phoenix.

JACK McDOWELL

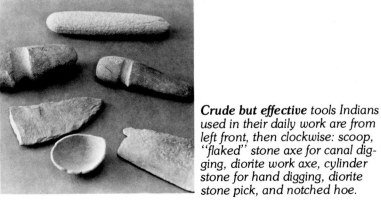

JACK McDOWELL

Crude but effective tools Indians used in their daily work are from left front, then clockwise: scoop, "flaked" stone axe for canal digging, diorite work axe, cylinder stone for hand digging, diorite stone pick, and notched hoe.

Colorado River Basin   141

The Salt in its Canyon
Moody, muddy, and running free

Below the confluence of the White and the Black rivers but above the damming, the Salt cuts a spectacular canyon. As the mood strikes, the Salt (silty in spring) rushes angrily or moves peacefully by. Sometimes it roars over a series of small falls. Thanks to a modern highway, the canyon is easily accessible. U.S. 60 gradually drops down five curving miles to the river, then bridges the water. Located halfway between Globe and Show Low, the river here is the boundary between the Fort Apache and the San Carlos Indian reservations.

JACK McDOWELL

Ocotillo nicely frames view of the Salt River Canyon. Looking downstream, the river bends back and forth between massive cliffs which change colors with the light of day. U.S. 60 snakes up and down the canyon and across the river. Off the main highway, a rough dirt road parallels for a short distance the north bank of the river. Near the bridge are a few picnic ramadas and a sandy beach.

Salt beds, downstream from the U.S. 60 crossing of the river and just below the confluence of Cibecue Creek and the Salt, are probably the reason for the river's name. A source of salt for local Indians until the 1940s, the beds give the river a brackish taste when the water is low.

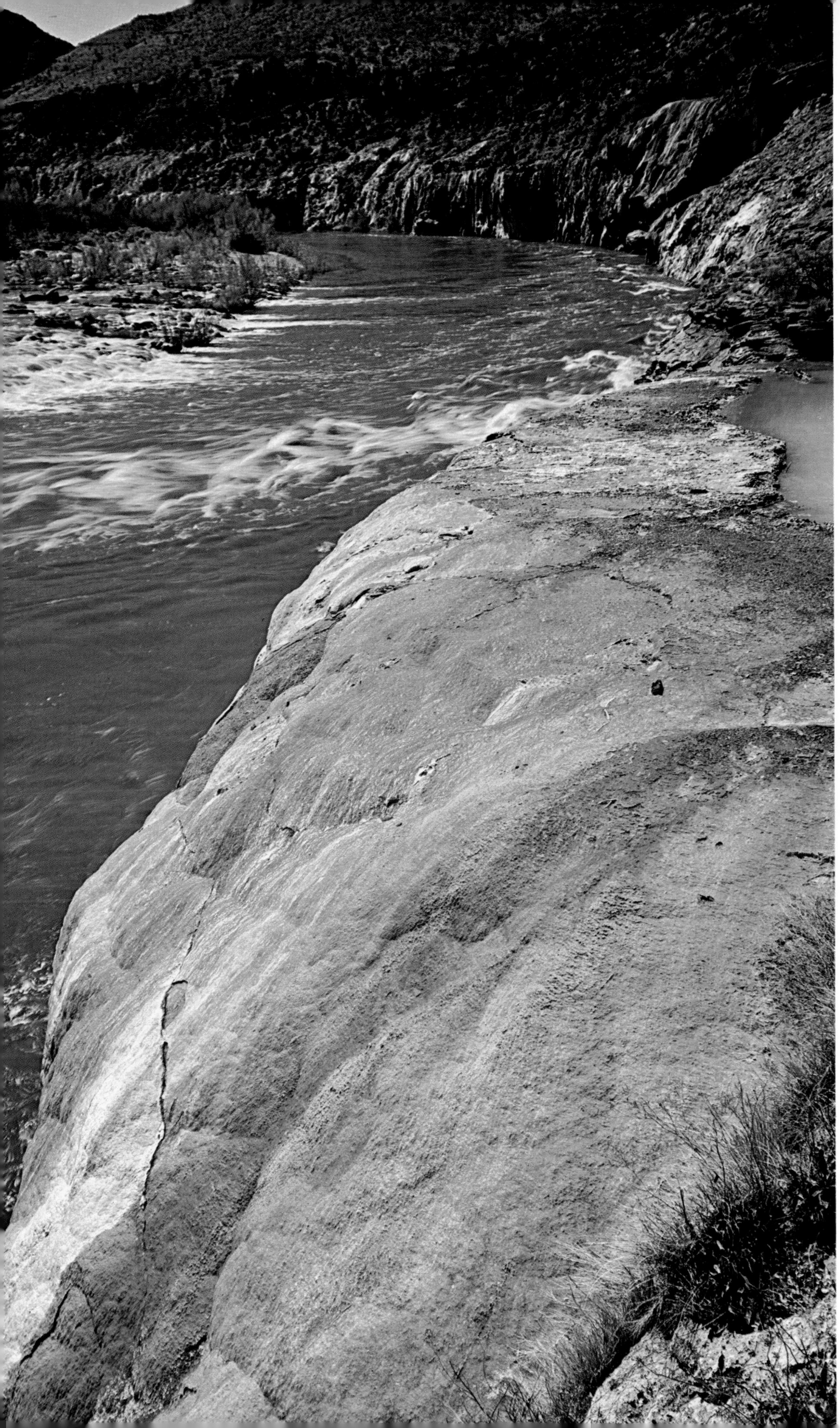

DAVID MUENCH

The Salt River
Harnessing the Salt
Bringing the river to town to stay

Control of the Salt River is crucial to Phoenix. Without its water, the desert city could not survive. But, keeping the city alive drains the river dry. Under the management of the Salt River Project, the river is caught in its early stages and held for year-round municipal, industrial, and agricultural use. The uppermost dam on the Salt is Roosevelt. Three more storage dams (all with hydroelectric plants) and two on the Verde regulate the river's water, which is delivered throughout the city by a 1,300-mile system of canals.

Roosevelt Lake, reservoir behind Roosevelt Dam, is the uppermost and the major storage facility for the Salt River Project. In addition, it is a popular recreational destination for desert water buffs. The snow-covered Sierra Anchas and cactus and sage-dotted canyon walls provide a dramatic backdrop for Roosevelt Lake.

Roosevelt Dam *is the key control on the Salt. Construction took place between 1905 and 1911, with mule-driven wagons transporting supplies 60 rugged miles from Mesa to the damsite. At the damsite, Italians busily quarried 350,000 cubic yards of stone cut from the side of the mountain; then they shaped, washed, and cemented the stone into place. Cresting at 280 feet, Roosevelt Dam, then and today, ranks as the highest masonry dam in the world. Here the spillway is going, a rare occurrence in this land of little rain.*

Colorado River Basin   145

...HARNESSING THE SALT

Main thoroughfares cross back and forth over canals (here the Grand).
Two main canals, beginning at Granite Reef Diversion Dam, and four
branch canals channel the water throughout Phoenix.

JACK McDOWELL

Siphon irrigation for crops is popular in the Phoenix area. One end of the siphon rests in a lateral canal, the other in a ditch in a field. Siphons inserted into a lateral fill with water. A farmer "caps" the other end to keep the water in the tube until the siphon is in the correct position. About 250,000 acres are under cultivation because of Salt River Project water. Main crops are lettuce, citrus, flowers, sugar beets, cotton, alfalfa, grains.

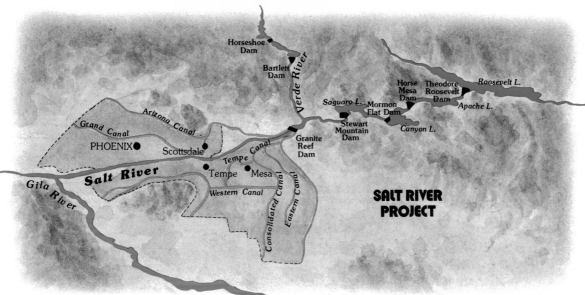

Salt River Project features: four storage dams and one diversion dam (Granite Reef) on the Salt, and a system of canals. After the "rainy" season, the river's bed is usually dry. Dotted area on map indicates the area serviced by the Salt River Project.

Lawn watering is unique in Phoenix. Lawns are flooded every 28 days in winter, every 14 days in summer. Residents sign up for water; a computer printout lists scheduled time and how much each customer gets. Water comes from a canal to the home via underground pipes.

Colorado River Basin   147

The Salt River

Apache Trail

Roller coaster road to tranquil waters

Carved through country as wild as its name, the Apache
Trail was laid out in 1905 for transporting materials from the
railroad at Mesa to the site of Roosevelt Dam. The trail,
running 76 miles from Apache Junction (30 miles east of
Phoenix) to Globe, remains rugged between Canyon and
Roosevelt lakes and should be driven with care. Narrow,
twisting, and unpaved, the road has numerous ups and
downs, especially in labyrinthian Fish Creek Canyon. The
route follows the path of the Salt, providing access to
Canyon, Apache, and Roosevelt lakes and good spots for
boating, swimming, camping, and picnicking.

JACK McDOWELL

Stops along the trail. *Miles of smooth water at Canyon, Apache, and Roosevelt lakes provide fishing and boating opportunities in a desert setting. Along the lake's shores are places for picnicking and camping. Fishermen* **(left)** *try for warm-water fish at Canyon Lake, while campers* **(below)** *discuss the day's events in a secluded spot next to Apache Lake.*

Zigzagging *along the 60 miles of man-made lakes on the Salt, the Apache Trail is most colorful in spring. Winter rains turn the shrubby cliffs green, and desert wildflowers bloom in all their glory. The trail, bordered by steep dropoffs and vertical walls, is rugged. This particular point is just a few curves below Roosevelt Dam.*

Colorado River Basin   149

More Rivers in the Colorado Basin

Dolores River. Rising in the San Miguel Mountains just west of the Continental Divide, the Dolores River flows southwest, then north through western Colorado, merging with the Colorado River right after crossing into Utah. A free-flowing river, the Dolores is paralleled by Colorado state highways 141 and 145 for a spell, but no major towns lie along its route.

LARRY SMITH

San Juan River. Running 400 miles from the Rocky Mountains to Lake Powell, the San Juan River passes through Navajo Country and the "Four Corners." Near its headwaters the river irrigates land on the Navajo Indian Reservation. West of Mexican Hat, Utah, the San Juan executes a series of meandering bends. Known as the Great Goosenecks, these bends are considered by geologists to be one of the finest examples of "entrenched meanders" anywhere in the world.

Gila River. Originating in the mountains of western New Mexico, the Gila journeys 630 miles across the Arizona desert. Along the way stand Indian ruins (Casa Grande and Gila Cliff Dwellings) and still active reservations (Gila Bend and San Carlos). Although the river's mouth is the Colorado River at the Arizona-California border, the river bed is generally dry west of Coolidge Dam.

ED COOPER

RAY ATKESON

Yampa River. Running untamed, the Yampa begins in the Rockies and ends at the Green within Dinosaur National Monument. Sandstone formations along the way expose faults and folds—evidence of the earth's forces at work. The Yampa's last 70 miles are floatable.

Gunnison River. Eleven of the Gunnison's 150 miles wind through Black Canyon of the Gunnison National Monument, where the river cuts a deep channel through hard granite and schist. Three dams, part of the Colorado River Storage Project, block the river for irrigation. The Gunnison's entire flow lies within the state of Colorado.

Colorado River Basin   151

THE PACIFIC
From the Mountains

JACK McDOWELL

COASTAL BASIN to the Sea

Tyee Rapids, Rogue River

Pacific Coastal Rivers are just what the basin name implies. They are waterways beginning in the mountains (mostly the Coast or Cascade ranges) and emptying either into a bay or into the Pacific Ocean directly. No one river forms the center of the system. Instead, the basin is composed of an assortment of unrelated waters.

The most extensive system in the Pacific Coastal Basin is that of the Sacramento and San Joaquin. Along with their Sierra-born tributaries, they drain a considerable area in California. Other basin standouts are the Klamath in Northern California, the Rogue in Oregon, and the Skagit in Washington.

Some of the rivers work hard. The Sacramento and San Joaquin are used extensively for irrigating the Central Valley. Their tributaries and the Skagit are tremendous sources of hydroelectric power.

Most of the rivers offer recreational rewards. The Sacramento and San Joaquin's tributaries are a major source of recreation for Californians. The Rogue offers good drift fishing, floating, or river scenics. The mouths of the rivers, with their proximity to the ocean, make them popular with fishermen. Rivers contained within parks, such as the Hoh, Queets, and Quinault in Olympic National Park and the Smith in Jedediah Smith State Park, host swimmers, hikers, picnickers, or campers.

With the exception of the Sacramento and San Joaquin rivers, no major cities lie along the paths of the coastal rivers.

(For a map of the Pacific Coastal Basin and its relation to the rest of the West, turn to either the inside front or back cover.)

Pacific Coastal Basin   153

THE SACRAMENTO & SAN JOAQUIN
Main Arteries in the Central Valley

The Sacramento winds lazily south; the San Joaquin moves north. Before merging at the Delta, they pass through California's agriculturally rich lands

RICHARD DAWSON

California's heartland is the Central Valley, and the Sacramento and San Joaquin rivers form the Central Valley's heart. The Sacramento, born in the Klamath Mountains, flows south for 400 miles; the San Joaquin originates in the Sierra Nevada Range and flows west for 125 miles before turning north for its final 175-mile run. The two rivers merge at the Delta.

The Sacramento and San Joaquin valleys are predominantly agricultural. During the late 1800s, the valley floors were covered chiefly with wheat, but, with the introduction of irrigation, the farm scene changed. Today, over 1 million acres of irrigated land produce about 200 different crops.

Irrigation not only changed the farming picture but also changed the course of the rivers. The San Joaquin River is blocked in its upper reaches and diverted south, away from its natural northern route. To replace the lost waters, the Sacramento is dammed and, through controlled releases, sent to replace the lost San Joaquin. Under the auspices of the Central Valley Project, canals, pumping plants, dams, and reservoirs are at work to make sure the valley is well watered.

Major cities include Sacramento, Stockton, and Fresno. Interstate 5 and State Highway 99 parallel both rivers on the west and east. County roads off these major thoroughfares veer close to the rivers.

Neither the Sacramento nor the San Joaquin are recreational rivers, although the Sacramento attracts fishermen. Recreational traffic does occur on the reservoirs, where water enthusiasts take to the man-made lakes to escape the valley's heat.

Split personality. For most of its 400 miles, the Sacramento River meanders peacefully through acres and acres of farmlands. A different Sacramento lies above Shasta Dam; when swollen by winter rains, it cuts a devastating path.

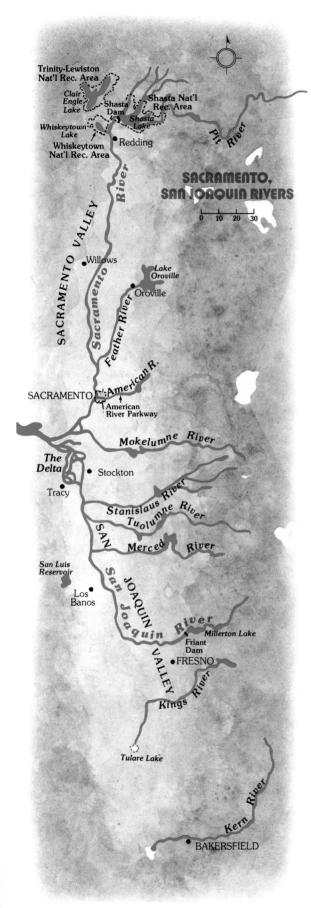

Trinity-Lewiston
Nat'l Rec. Area

Clair Engle Lake

Shasta Dam

Shasta Nat'l Rec. Area

Shasta Lake

Whiskeytown Lake

Whiskeytown Nat'l Rec. Area

● Redding

Pit River

SACRAMENTO, SAN JOAQUIN RIVERS

0   10   20   30

SACRAMENTO VALLEY

Sacramento River

● Willows

Lake Oroville

● Oroville

Feather River

American R.

SACRAMENTO

American River Parkway

Mokelumne River

The Delta

● Stockton

● Tracy

Stanislaus River

Tuolumne River

SAN

Merced River

San Luis Reservoir

Los Banos

SAN JOAQUIN River

JOAQUIN VALLEY

Millerton Lake

Friant Dam

● FRESNO

Kings River

Tulare Lake

Kern River

● BAKERSFIELD

Major sport on the valley rivers is fishing the Sacramento, with autumn steelhead and salmon runs bringing anglers out in droves. More relaxed fishermen take to the Delta **(below)** or to the Sacramento or Stockton deep-water channels.

Sacramento City and River

The jumping-off place for the diggings

California's famed gold rush of 1849 put Sacramento —river and city—on the map. Vessels jammed with eager prospectors steamed up river from the San Francisco area to Sacramento City. From Sacramento City newly outfitted miners set off on foot, mule, or boat for the diggings along the Feather, Yuba, Bear, and American rivers. Strategically located midway between the northern mines and the San Francisco area, Sacramento City boomed as the inland supply center for the northern mining camps.

SACRAMENTO CITY AND COUNTY MUSEUM

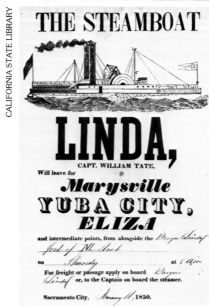

CALIFORNIA STATE LIBRARY

THE STEAMBOAT

LINDA,
CAPT. WILLIAM TATE.

Will leave for

Marysville

YUBA CITY,
ELIZA

and intermediate points, from alongside the *Barque Lindsay foot of M Street*

on *Thursday* at *8 a.m.*

For freight or passage apply on board *Barque Lindsay* or, to the Captain on board the steamer.

Sacramento City, *January 11,* 1850.

Sacramento's waterfront in 1849 *(above)*, as depicted in the George V. Cooper lithograph, looked humble but bustled with activity. Simple wood-frame buildings on the embarcadero housed day-to-day activities, wagons busily transported merchandise from one place to another, and river boats arrived or departed with goods, gold, or enthusiastic prospectors. Handbills, such as the one at **left**, were posted about town announcing the departure of a steamer for the diggings.

PADDLE WHEELERS ON WESTERN WATERS

The song "Waiting for the Robert E. Lee," Mark Twain's tales of the Mississippi, Robert Fulton, Edna Ferber's classic novel *Show Boat*—all these bring to mind the proud paddle wheel steamboat, with its ever-turning wheel, distinctive whistle, and continuous trail of steam. Although paddle wheelers most often are associated with eastern waters, they were not unique to the East. Their existence hasn't been immortalized in song, story, or history text, but paddle boats did ply western waters.

The discovery of gold in 1848 beckoned the paddle wheeler to the West—some 40 years after its eastern appearance. From San Francisco, prospectors and supplies were paddled up the Sacramento to the gold fields and mining camps; bags of nuggets came downstream. Because of the success of the paddle wheeler as a means of transportation, builders materialized overnight, creating more boats than there were passengers. The once $45 to $65 ride upstream could be had for a mere 10 cents. To bring order to chaos, the boat owners consolidated, forming the California Steam Navigation Company.

One of the most heralded paddle wheelers of the West plied the Sacramento. The Chrysopolis, built in 1860 to rival the "floating palaces" of the East, had wheels as tall as a three-story house, a crisp white exterior, and an elegant interior of polished brass and red velvet. Capacity was 1,000 passengers and 700 tons of freight.

Steamboating on the Sacramento was short lived. Competition from railroads was stiff, and hydraulic mining clogged river channels. In 1871 the California Steam Navigation Company sold its fleet to the California Pacific Railroad.

Paddle wheelers arrived on the "unnavigable" Colorado in 1852 when Captain George Johnson

was contracted by the government to deliver supplies to Fort Yuma, 150 boulder-packed, shallow miles upstream from the river's mouth. With the discovery of minerals along the banks of the Colorado in 1855 and with miners seeking fresh grounds, the river became a refuge for people hoping to strike it rich. Increase in activity on the river prompted the government to send Lieutenant Joseph C. Ives to find the Colorado's upstream navigation point, which proved to be Black Canyon (site of Hoover Dam).

The nature of the river made movement on the Colorado slow and difficult. Navigation was never attempted at night because of the ever changing river channel. The railroad, with its ability to provide more efficient service, put the steamboat second in demand. In 1878 the Colorado Steam Navigation Company sold out to Southern Pacific.

Settlements had already been established on the Columbia (and Willamette) in 1850 when the paddle wheeler made its appearance, transporting supplies and goods on weekly runs between Astoria, Vancouver, Portland, and Oregon City. River traffic really boomed in the 1860s when the gold rush was on in Idaho and Canada.

The Columbia's falls and rapids made it necessary to navigate the river in sections. First leg on the 229-mile Portland to Wallula trip, operated by the Oregon Steam Navigation Company, was a six-hour ride to the Cascades. Passengers and freight were railroaded around the Cascades' rapids to steamers which took them to The Dalles for an overnight stop. Early the next morning, passengers departed on a 1½-hour train trip around the falls to above Celilo, where another steamer left for Wallula—the embarkation point for Boise, Salt Lake, or points east.

Eventually the mines gave out and the paddle wheelers returned to hauling grain. Although they would continue to play an active role on the Columbia for another generation, as on the Sacramento and the Colorado, the paddle wheeler lost out as a primary means of transportation.

T. J. Potter on the Columbia River around 1905.

The Sacramento and San Joaquin
California's Farm Belt
Massive irrigation nurtures 200 crops

The advent of irrigation completely changed the agricultural scene in the Sacramento and San Joaquin valleys. Before 1890, grain, dependent only on rain for water, covered both valleys. After 1890, developers brought in water, and ranchers banded together to form irrigation districts. Large ranches were broken down into smaller ones, and fruit orchards, alfalfa, vegetable crops, and vineyards were planted. Later came cotton, rice, sugar beets, and pastureland. Lying in the San Joaquin Valley are Fresno, Tulare, and Kern counties, the three richest agricultural counties in the nation. Ensuring the valleys of enough water for their farmlands are the Central Valley Project and the California State Water Project.

TED STRESHINSKY

Table grape country. Stretching endlessly across the San Joaquin Valley, particularly in Fresno County, are rows and rows of grape vines. The San Joaquin Valley is not only the heart of California's grape growing industry, but it is also the holder of the three richest agricultural counties in the nation—Fresno, Tulare, and Kern.

Marked contrast to the geomet. order of tilled fields are flooded ri fields. Low levees surrounding th fields twist and turn following th contour of the land. Rice is sou from the air in late spring, then t fields are flooded. In the fall th are drained, and the rice harvested and sent to drie California produces one-fifth of t nation's rice, with 90 per cent that crop coming from the low Sacramento Valle

A drink of water. *Because walnut trees require more water than winter rains supply, walnut growers rely on irrigation. Lateral canals channel water to individual fields where siphons transfer the water from the ditch to the orchard. Walnut groves cover the lower San Joaquin Valley.*

JACK McDOWELL

One of California's biggest crops. Cotton likes the hot climate and availability of water in the lower Central Valley, especially in Kern County. The Kern River doesn't carry enough water to support crops growing on the surrounding lands so the San Joaquin River is sent south through the Friant-Kern Canal to give the Kern a boost.

The Sacramento and San Joaquin
Controls on the Valley Rivers
Sending the Sacramento to boost the San Joaquin

Though the majority of water is in the Sacramento Valley, the bulk of irrigable lands are in the San Joaquin Valley. Adjusting this imbalance and ensuring water at the right place and at the right time is the purpose of the Central Valley Project, operated by the Bureau of Reclamation. Shasta Dam blocks the upper Sacramento, Friant Dam blocks the San Joaquin. The Friant-Kern Canal carries the water south to Kern County. To replace the San Joaquin's lost flow, the Sacramento is captured in its upper reaches, sent across the Delta, and pumped into the San Joaquin Valley. In addition to irrigation, other benefits are flood control, hydroelectric power, recreational reservoirs, and waterfowl refuges.

JACK McDOWELL

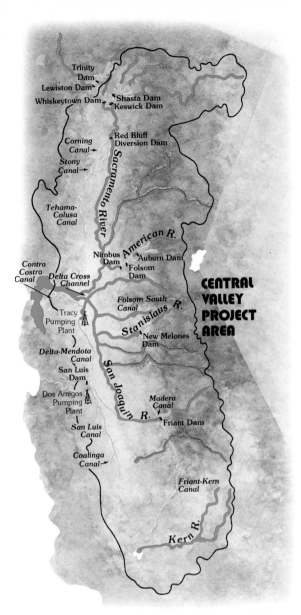

STORAGE RESERVOIRS

CAPACITY
ACRE FEET

CLAIR ENGLE		
TOTAL	2 4 4 8 0 0 0	
CURRENT	2 3 6 6 0 0 0	
WHISKEYTOWN		
TOTAL	2 4 1 0 0 0	
CURRENT	2 2 2 9 0 0	
SHASTA		
TOTAL	4 5 5 2 0 0 0	
CURRENT	4 1 8 8 3 0 0	
AUBURN		
TOTAL	2 3 2 9 0 0 0	
CURRENT		
FOLSOM		
TOTAL	1 0 1 0 0 0 0	
CURRENT	6 7 1 7 0 0	
SAN LUIS		
TOTAL	2 0 4 1 0 0 0	
CURRENT	1 9 9 7 3 0 0	
NEW HOGAN		
TOTAL	3 2 4 0 0 0	
CURRENT	2 2 3 3 0 0	
NEW MELONES		
TOTAL	2 4 0 0 0 0 0	
CURRENT		
MILLERTON		
TOTAL	5 2 0 5 0 0	
CURRENT	4 5 2 3 0 0	
BLACK BUTTE		
TOTAL	1 6 0 0 0 0	
CURRENT	9 7 2 0 0	
BERRYESSA		
TOTAL	1 6 0 2 0 0 0	
CURRENT	1 6 2 5 7 0 0	

Dams and canals throughout the Central Valley block and store excess river water, then channel it to where it is needed. Under the direction of the Central Valley Project, Shasta Dam blocks the upper Sacramento; Friant Dam blocks the San Joaquin. At the Tracy Pumping Plant, the Sacramento is lifted into the San Joaquin Valley. Across the Delta is a cross channel.

Keeping tabs on Central Valley Project operating facilities is the Water and Power Control Division Operations Center in Sacramento. Data from branch offices is assembled, correlated, and analyzed to make sure all systems are working together. Graphs and lights lining one wall of the center illustrate the status of all project operations—from water level of reservoirs to amount of energy being generated.

At the point of transfer. In the Delta-Mendota Canal, the Sacramento River enters the San Joaquin Valley. From here it is channeled and distributed throughout the water-deficient San Joaquin Valley.

JACK McDOWELL

Pacific Coastal Basin   **163**

Storage reservoirs *turn into recreational lakes for thousands of Californians during the summer, as swimmers, water-skiers, sailors, power boaters, houseboaters, and campers flock to the lake of their choice. Of the 23 reservoirs in the Central Valley system, Shasta and Folsom lakes are the most heavily used. Millerton draws big crowds in the hot and dry southern portion of the valley. Trinity Lake* ***(above)*** *lies in the evergreen belt, and, at 2,370 feet, is just high enough to escape the scorching valley heat.*

...CONTROLS ON VALLEY RIVERS

Marsh lands *have been created in the Sacramento Valley with Central Valley Project water to provide migratory waterfowl with a place to rest, nest, and feed. The wildlife refuges replace wetlands reduced in area by agricultural activities, protect waterfowl from hunters, and discourage the birds from feeding at freshly sown fields. The busiest time of year at the refuges is November through February.*

Waterfowl...home is where the river is

Wild ducks and swans frequent the upper Snake, and osprey nest along Idaho's St. Joe. But the really intense concentrations of various waterfowl are found October through February at the national wildlife refuges along the Pacific Flyway. Millions of birds wing their way south each year over the central valleys of Washington, Oregon, and California. They are attracted to marsh lands along the upper Sacramento, but the most popular stopping spot is the Klamath-Tule Lake region on the California-Oregon border. Damming of the rivers has prevented flooding which created the coveted wetlands. National wildlife refuges are now recreating this type of environment so that waterfowl will have a place to nest, feed, and rest.

DOUG WILSON LINDA COHEN

Osprey leaves nest in search of food. A fish-eating species of hawk, ospreys have a wing span of 4½ to 6 feet, nest in dead snags, and bear and raise their young from April to September.

Trumpeter swans ruffle their snow white feathers while courting. Mating is for life; when one dies, the other does too—of a broken heart. Named for the clarion-like sounds they make while flying, trumpeter swans dip their long, curving necks into the water in search of food.

Canada geese (top) flap their wings as they head south along the Pacific Flyway. Although the goldeneye duck (middle) doesn't migrate, he takes off for an adventure close to home. Taking a more leisurely approach to life is this family of mallards (left), out for an afternoon swim.

Pacific Coastal Basin   167

The Sacramento and San Joaquin
At Sacramento and Stockton
Ports of call serving the valley

Up-river ports at Sacramento and Stockton serve the needs
of the Central Valley. Stockton's port, the older of the two
and in existence since 1933, has space for 13 vessels. It
exports agricultural products from the valley and mineral
ores from the western United States. The Port of
Sacramento has berths for five ships and container loading
facilities; it exports mainly bulk rice, wood chips, chemicals,
and feed grains. Both ports are reached through deep-water
channels, with Sacramento 79 and Stockton 75 nautical
miles away from the Golden Gate Bridge.

JACK McDOWELL

*Stockton to Japan. Coke bound
for the Orient is being loaded on
the Nebula at the Port of Stockton.
Of special interest is the SS
California, which uses Stockton as
its base. Carrying more than 2.5
million gallons of bulk wines from
the Central Valley to bottling plants
on the Atlantic coast, the ship
becomes a floating wine cellar.*

Unlikely companions. Sailboa
move about in Sacramento
deep-water channel on balm
weekends, while an ocean-goin
vessel, docked at the port, awai
loading or unloading. The Port
Sacramento, specializing in bu
handling, has facilities to loa
bulk rice, grain, and feed com
modities on board a ship at th
rate of up to 600 tons an hou

American River Parkway

A natural corridor through the heart of Sacramento

The last 30 miles of the American River, from below
Nimbus Dam to the Sacramento River, are not very
exciting. The river moves rather slowly, with only a couple
of short patches of fast water. Vegetation is typically
cottonwoods and willows. But the charm of the American
River Parkway is that it runs, unnoticed except to those who
know it's there, through the metropolitan areas of
Sacramento County, creating a variety of park and
river-oriented activities for city dwellers.

JACK McDOWELL

Spirited game of ball takes place in tree-shaded spot in Ancil Hoffman Park. Other patches of green within the parkway are Discovery and C. M. Goethe parks.

Water enthusiasts portage innertubes along rocky beach to the beginning of the rapids. A fast stretch begins at C. M. Goethe Park. The ride down and portage back takes about 25 minutes.

Bridle paths (and hiking and biking trails) follow the river bank through much of the parkway and, in a few places, even ford the river.

Pacific Coastal Basin   171

The Sacramento and San Joaquin

The Delta

A maze of meandering waterways

Sloughs, islands, farmlands, small towns, waterways—all comprise the Delta, the meeting place of the Sacramento and San Joaquin rivers. Containing about 740,000 acres (of which 50,000 are water), the Delta attracts fishing and boating enthusiasts. Planned but not as yet constructed is the Peripheral Canal, destined to carry water along the eastern side of the Delta. Water in turn would be released at various places into the Delta. Points in favor of the canal are more control over the amount and quality of the water, while opponents are for preserving the Delta's natural state.

PORT OF SACRAMENTO

An incongruous sight—farmer and freighter share the Delta. Although the ocean-going vessel seems to be gliding over the fields, it is simply passing through one of the Delta's many waterways. Dredging has restored the original navigability of the channels, providing ocean-going vessels a water route between the Pacific Ocean and Stockton's and Sacramento's deep-water channels. Although agriculture is not as big on the Delta as in past years, the islands still have their share of farmlands. Irrigation is simple—the lifting of the levee gates immerses the field.

ELLS MARUGG

JACK McDOWELL

Wandering waterways *move through the Delta's flat countryside. Originally a densely forested inland everglade, the Delta's banks were denuded by the furnaces of earlyday river boats. Later, the land was transformed into levee-rimmed islands that produced fortunes in asparagus and fruit for Delta farmers.*

Recreation is big *on the Delta. Houseboating is a leisurely way to explore the innumerable channels. Stops can be made at Delta towns, such as Isleton and Walnut Grove, or at one of the state recreation areas. The Delta also receives heavy use from fishermen, power boaters, and water-skiers.*

THE SIERRA RIVERS
They Offer Something for Everyone

Making fast trips from the mountains to the valley, these rivers pause long enough to stock Californians with water, power, and recreation

Sierra rivers—major ones being the Feather, American, Mokelumne, Stanislaus, Tuolumne, Merced, and Kings—are born in the tremendous snow pack of the Sierra Nevada. Fed by small streams and numerous waterfalls during spring thaw, they surge down the western slope of the mountains on their way to their meeting with either the Sacramento or the San Joaquin rivers in the Central Valley. (The Kings—an exception—ends in dry Tulare Lake.) Their journeys are short, averaging 60 to 100 miles, but their flows are used wisely and well by Californians.

These rivers abound with recreational opportunities. You can ride the thrilling rapids of the Stanislaus and Tuolumne, walk along the bank of the bubbling Merced in Yosemite National Park, camp along the North Fork of the Feather, strike out for the primitive Middle Fork of the Feather, picnic at a state park along the Merced, sail on a reservoir on the Mokelumne, or simply marvel at the beauty of the Kings in Kings Canyon National Park.

But the value of the Sierra rivers goes beyond recreation. The Central Valley Project operates Folsom Dam and Reservoir on the American River; the California State Water Project relies on Oroville Dam and Lake Oroville; Hetch Hetchy Reservoir on the Tuolumne supplies the city and county of San Francisco with water; and Pacific Gas and Electric power plants on numerous Sierra streams send electricity to northern and central California homes.

Also to their credit, the Sierra rivers have a lasting place in the annals of history. For it was in 1848 in the American River that James Marshall discovered gold.

One-lane wooden bridge, held together by wooden pegs, crosses the Stanislaus River at Knights Ferry. This covered bridge built in 1864 replaced the original structure that was swept away by the destructive floods of 1862. By the time the Stanislaus reaches Knights Ferry, the river has dropped considerably on its journey from the Sierra to the valley, but the massive boulders so typical of Sierra rivers are still much in evidence.

A fisherman's delight is a twelve-inch rainbow fresh from the Stanislaus River. The clear, cool waters of Sierra-born rivers harbor schools of trout, for these rivers are not as heavily fished as the natural and man-made lakes.

Pacific Coastal Basin   175

The American River
Gold Fever!
Still around...a century after The Rush

In January, 1848, James Marshall rocked the world when he discovered in the American River "some kind of mettle . . . that looks like goald . . ." Loud and clear went out the cry that gold—as much as was wanted—was waiting in the foothills of California. Fortune hunters flocked to the west by the thousands, and mining camps sprang up overnight along the Feather, Yuba, Bear, Tuolumne, Merced, American, Stanislaus, Mokelumne, and Calaveras rivers. Eventually, the gold ran out, and the miners deserted the Sierra camps for greener pastures. But the get-rich-quick spirit that moved the forty-niners still survives.

TOM MYERS

Weekend miners search for gold with a long rectangular box, similar to the rockers, Long Toms, and/or sluice boxes used by the forty-niners. Dirt is poured into the top. Large rocks are caught in the sieve, waste runs out through the lower end with the water, and the heavy gold falls to the bottom of the box. These miners are working the American River near Coloma, the original gold discovery site.

Like their forefathers, youngste pan for gold in the Sierra river Panning, a slow but easy metho is a sifting process in which water used to float off lighter materi while heavy, gold-bearing particle settle. The best conditions fo "panning" are found in spring ar summer, when the rivers are fu

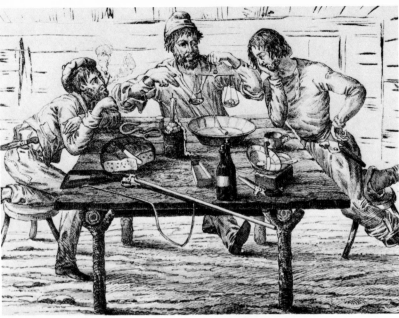

Golddiggers of 1849. *Life in the mines was anything but glamourous. The necessities of day-to-day living were hard to come by and expensive. But, when miners had gold to weigh, hardships were temporarily disregarded and gaiety took over.*

JACK McDOWELL

The Merced, Stanislaus, and Kings

In the Parks

Rivers easy to reach, easy to enjoy

A few stretches of Sierra-born rivers are high enough in elevation to have that mountain flavor but are not so high that they are difficult to reach. And once you get to them, the rivers can be enjoyed with the greatest of ease. Falling nicely into this category are the Merced River in the valley of Yosemite National Park, the Stanislaus River in Calaveras Big Trees State Park, and the Kings River in Kings Canyon National Park.

TED STRESHINSKY

In Yosemite Valley, *visitors are more inclined to bike **(top of page)** or hike along or across the Merced River than actually to take a plunge. But summertime finds an occasional fisherman braving the chilly waters.*

Cool, green waters *of the Stanislaus in Calaveras Big Trees State Park are paradise on hot summer days. In some places small waterfalls create swimming basins; in others, boulders cluttering the river provide good sun sitting spots. Edging the river is glacier-carved granite, so typical of Sierra rivers.*

P.G.&E. goes into the high country of the Sierra several times during winter to measure the snow's water content. This enables the company, in cooperation with state agencies, to predict the amount of spring runoff that will be available for hydroelectric generation and for downstream agricultural irrigation. The information also helps state agencies to forecast potential flooding conditions.

CALIFORNIA'S "POWER-FULL" RIVERS

When northern and central Californians turn on their lights, electric stoves, stereos, or plug in their shavers, chances are that the energy is coming from a Pacific Gas and Electric Company hydroelectric plant on a Sierra or Cascade river.

The use of the Sierra rivers for power dates back to the 1850s and the introduction of hydraulic mining in the Sierra foothills. The idea of using water to produce energy spread through Northern California communities, starting in 1887 at Grass Valley and Nevada City. Soon, numerous small companies were in the "power" business.

It soon became evident that more efficient service could be provided by larger companies with substantial capital. Beginning in 1905 several of the small electric power producers merged to form Pacific Gas and Electric Company.

Today the largest private supplier of power in the United States, P.G.&E. serves 2.8 million electric customers in 47 California counties from hydroelectric plants at 65 locations (mostly on rivers in the Sierra) and 12 thermal plants.

Sierra rivers producing power are the Feather, Mokelumne, Yuba, Bear, American, Merced, Kings, Kern, Stanislaus, Tule, Calaveras, and Tuolumne as well as the Pit, Eel, San Joaquin, Sacramento, and Trinity.

Besides producing energy, power dams play a key role in flood control and water conservation. Another benefit is recreation on storage reservoirs.

As the need for energy continues to increase and because building dams in the Sierra is no longer economically feasible, P.G.&E. is now working on the recycling principle. The company is planning a pumped-storage project on the Kings River. After water passes through a power plant planned at Courtright Reservoir, it will be stored at Lake Wishon. Instead of passing into the Kings River, the water will be pumped back into Lake Courtright during off-peak hours to be used again.

A King of Kings. The South Fork of the Kings River in Kings Canyon National Park is truly regal. A foaming, frothy, fast-moving river, it drops 2,000 feet in elevation within just a few miles. A Motor Nature Trail that parallels and crosses the river and a footbridge and 1½-mile-long trail in Zumwalt Meadow put you close to the Kings. Below the park, the river, held in Pine Flat Reservoir, irrigates acres of land in the Central Valley. Although the Kings is considered part of the San Joaquin drainage, it rarely reaches the San Joaquin River. Normally, it ends in dry Tulare Lake.

JACK McDOWELL

The Tuolumne River and the Feather's Middle Fork
The Pristine Areas
Challenging to explore...delightful rewards

The primitive state of the Middle Fork of the Feather has been preserved with its inclusion in the Wild and Scenic Rivers Act, 1968. Generally inaccessible, especially in the upper canyon wild river stretch, the Middle Fork provides unspoiled and unpeopled spots for fishing, hiking, or simply enjoying the wilderness. The Tuolumne River above Hetch Hetchy Reservoir in Yosemite National Park flows through an exquisite meadow before falling rapidly through its grand canyon. The only way to experience the upper Tuolumne, reachable just in summer, is on foot.

TED STRESHINSKY

Hiking bold and fearless. Backpackers head for Glen Aulin High Sierra Camp, the best place to begin exploring the Grand Canyon of the Tuolumne River.

Feather River Country. A half-day round trip hike through timbered lands and across creeks in Plumas National Forest leads to an overlook and a deep view of the Feather's Middle Fork. The trail has its ups and downs, but the worst "up" is the last mile out.

The Feather's Middle Fork
...PRISTINE AREAS

Scenic but rugged *Milsap Bar on the Middle Fork of the Feather lies in the midst of a pine and fir-studded canyon. Clear, bluish-green waters offer a refreshing retreat on hot summer days and good trout fishing. Madrone leaves carpet a small campground on the east bank of the river.*

TED STRESHINSKY

There's a reward for the adventuresome fisherman—trout bite within minutes. The wild portion of the Feather's Middle Fork is a fisherman's paradise because it is almost inaccessible and therefore little fished. Access point to boulder-strewn stretch is Stag Point. A gravel, one-lane road from Stag Point to the river is not for the faint of heart—dropping 3,000 feet in two miles.

Feather Falls on the Feather's Middle Fork is the third highest waterfall (640 feet) in the United States. To reach the feathery fall, follow a 3½-mile trail through a forest of evergreens and lush ferns to an overlook perched on top of a pinnacle 1,900 feet above the river's bed.

The Stanislaus and Tuolumne
Riding the Rapids
In California—white water at its best

Some of the most exciting white water belongs to the Tuolumne. The runable stretch, just south of Yosemite National Park, has the fastest drop—an average of 45 feet per mile—of any river in the West. Flowing through a primitive canyon, the clear, cold waters churn more than 65 times in about 22 miles, one rapid stretching more than a mile long. On the other side of the scale, the Stanislaus offers an excellent introduction to white water. A nine-mile ride through a remote canyon in the Mother Lode country introduces you to about 20 easy but thrilling rapids. Between 30,000 and 40,000 people float the Stanislaus annually, making it a most heavily run river.

PHYLLIS ELVING

At day's end, clothes dry on a conveniently located branch, sleeping bags rest on a flat stretch of sandy beach, and a fisherman casts his line for rainbows. Mealtimes are informal gatherings around the campfire.

Going under! You'll get dunked in the ice-cold rapids of the Tuolumne River time and again, but experienced oarsmen know how to keep rubber rafts under control. A ride on the Tuolumne is a guaranteed first-class white-water trip. The nature of the river, the canyon it flows through, and regulations (permits required) by the National Forest Service make running the Tuolumne a true wilderness experience.

The Feather River
Reworking California's Rivers
Goal: get needed water to the dry southland

Three-fourths of California's water is in the northern one-third of the state; 75 per cent of the water needs are in the southern two-thirds of the state. To correct that imbalance and transport water 650 miles down state, the people of California approved in 1960 the construction of the California State Water Project. Initial facilities include 18 reservoirs, 15 pumping plants, 5 power plants, and 580 miles of aqueduct. Project water now irrigates 500,000 areas of formerly unusable land on the west side of the San Joaquin Valley and keeps Southern California in water for home, factory, and farm use. Additional benefits include smog-free electric power, flood control, and recreation.

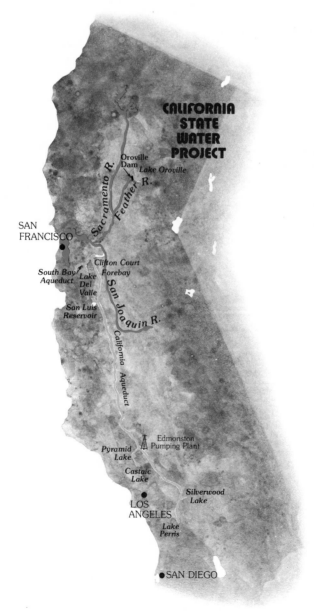

NORMAN A. PLATE

Biking enthusiasts can sample the California Aqueduct in three places. A 67-mile stretch runs between Tracy and Los Banos; a 41-mile and 28-mile bikeway parallel the aqueduct in Southern California's Antelope Valley.

Key features of the state water project are Oroville Dam (capturing the great flow of the Feather), San Luis Reservoir (storing the water south of the Delta), and the aqueducts (delivering water where it is needed).

Serpentining down Antelope Valley, the California Aqueduct carries life-giving water to the parched lands and people-packed cities of Southern California. The concrete-lined aqueduct runs for 444 miles from the Sacramento-San Joaquin Delta to Perris Reservoir in Riverside County. Not expected to reach capacity until about the year 2010, the aqueduct is in some places wide and deep enough to hold an ocean-going vessel. At the Tehachapi Mountains, the barrier separating northern and southern California, the water gets a 1,926 foot lift from fourteen 80,000 horsepower pumps at the Edmonston Pumping Plant.

THE COASTAL RIVERS
Colorfully Named...Little Used

Taking short but scenic trips from the mountains to the sea, the coastal streams are high in number, low in volume

The number of rivers rising in the Coast or Cascade ranges and flowing directly into the ocean is quite large. For example, there's the seasonal Salinas, the Mad, Mattole, Russian, Klamath, Eel, and Smith in California. In Oregon there's the Rogue, Coquille, Umpqua, Siuslaw, Yaquina, Siletz, and the Nehalem. Washington has the Hoh, Queets, Quinault, Soleduck, Green, Snoqualmie, Skykomish, Stillaguamish, and the Skagit.

Although the rivers' names are certainly colorful, very few are well known or heavily relied upon. Most journey just a short distance—their paths crossed only by motorists whizzing over U. S. Highway 101 along the coast.

Several rivers do stand out. The Skagit, Washington's most important coastal river, is dammed in its upper reaches to provide hydroelectric power for the Seattle area. In Oregon, it's the Rogue. More a recreational river than a working river, the Rogue beckons fishermen, rafters, and boaters. Part of the Rogue (and part of its tributary, the Illinois) are included in the federal Wild and Scenic Rivers Act.

California's best known rivers are the Eel, Klamath, and Russian. The Eel, considered an excellent fishing stream, makes news almost annually when it overflows its banks. The Russian is known in summer for massive numbers of canoers and in the winter for the havoc it causes during heavy winter rains. Largest by far, the Klamath River is a frantic place during fall salmon runs. Salmon are not the only "runners" of the Klamath. Commercial operators run float trips on the river in summer.

DICK DAWSON

Favorite summer pastime for many Northern Californians, canoeing down the Russian River can be almost as hectic as tackling rush-hour freeway traffic. Warm days, cool and calm waters, and the river's accessibility to the San Francisco Bay area make one-day canoe trips on the Russian popular.

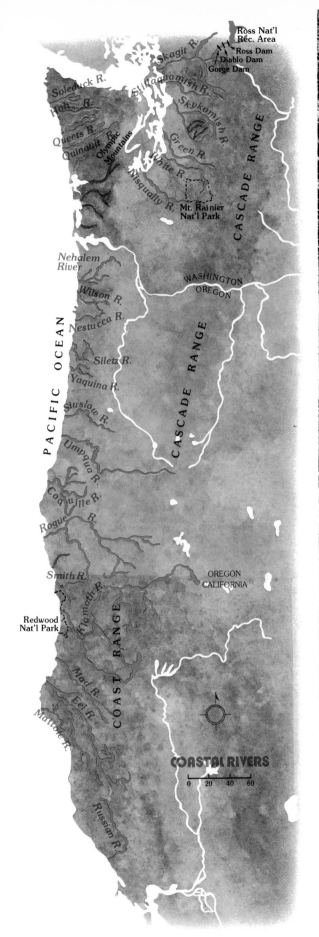

Rivers and redwoods *prevail along Northern California's coast. Although the rivers are not as well known as the redwoods, they offer excellent opportunities for fishing and leisurely recreation. Within many state parks along the rivers, hiking trails follow or cross the water as this one does along the Smith River in Jedediah Smith State Park.*

Pacific Coastal Basin   191

The Klamath, Russian, Eel, and Smith
Along the Northern California Coast
These rivers are strictly for fun

The lower reaches of the Russian, Eel, Smith, and Klamath are probably the best known and the most heavily used sections of Northern California's coastal rivers. Although the personalities of these rivers are not as dominating as the nearby Pacific and the surrounding towering redwoods, they have an identity of their own. And their main concern is outdoor fun. You can swim and raft at some spots, fish for salmon and steelhead, or simply hike along or picnic beside the water. Generally the rivers flow freely—the Russian and the Eel *too* freely during heavy rains, causing damaging floods. In its upper basin, the Klamath is dammed for irrigation, and an hydroelectric plant sits on the Eel.

JACK McDOWELL

JACK McDOWELL

Elbow-to-elbow fishermen—that's the mouth of the Klamath River during the fall king salmon run. Avid anglers eagerly await word that the salmon are biting and then converge on the river to cast from shore or troll from a boat. Although the Klamath kings migrate in both spring and fall, the fall migration is by far superior, accounting for a healthy percentage of the 168,000 salmon that enter the river annually. Kings average about 12 pounds, although their weight can range from 2 to 28 pounds. Steelhead swim the Klamath from September to April. Good steelhead runs are also found in the Mad, Russian, Mattole, Eel, and Smith rivers.

RECKLESS RIVERS— MOSTLY TAMED

Occasionally a western river will go on a rampage, overflowing its channels and leaving death and destruction in its wake. But, since construction began in the 1930s of multipurpose storage dams on innumerable rivers, the threat of floods has been greatly diminished.

What causes rivers to overrun their banks? The main reasons are excessive rain, rapid snow melt, or a cloudburst. Man has acted to curb the forces of nature by building dams that hold back unexpected heavy water flows. Levees have been built, vegetation has been planted along river banks in flood-prone areas to help absorb excess river flow, and river channels are kept as free as possible of logs and debris.

The classic example of an uncontrollable river was the Colorado. Before Hoover Dam was built in the early 1930s, the Colorado ran wild during spring Rocky Mountain snow melt. The Salton Sea, once a dry sink, is evidence of a two-year Colorado River rampage in 1905-07.

The Columbia and Snake rivers and their tributaries have ended their reckless days, now that a series of dams blocks their paths. Although no dam sits on the Willamette, dams on tributaries and on its two contributing forks control the once unpredictable river.

Oroville Dam, on California's Feather River, keeps the residents of Marysville and Yuba City resting easier—especially those who remember the devastating path the Feather cut in December, 1955. Other rivers originating in the western slope of the Sierra Nevada are under control, contained behind hydroelectric power dams.

Although the Sacramento River is tame below Shasta Dam, the river still cuts a disastrous path above the dam when heavy winter rains swell its flow and cause it to exceed its banks. And where the Sacramento and San Joaquin meet at the Delta, levee breakage and high water cause periodic flooding.

Notorious for overflowing their banks are the Eel and the Russian rivers along the Northern California coast. This situation has made the Eel River controversial. Should the river be dammed to prevent the disasterous floods, or should the river be allowed to remain free? A moratorium has been placed on dam building on the Eel until 1985. Until then, when the river will be reexamined, the Eel remains in California's wild rivers program.

Aftermath of a flood. Mailman, milkman, and drivers and riders of 10 more vehicles take pontoon ferry across the mouth of the Klamath. Debris and the raging waters of the Klamath swept away two of the bridge's five spans during the December, 1955, rampage.

Perhaps the most heavily canoed river in the West, the Russian (above) is paddled from Asti to the Alexander Valley Bridge by scores of San Francisco Bay Area residents during the summer. On the other hand, the Smith River, host to an annual raft race at Gasquet (right) draws more of a local crowd. Both rivers have seasonal flows, but Pacific Gas and Electric hydroelectric developments on the Eel send surplus water to the Russian, keeping it in business year round. During very rainy winters, the Russian is notorious for heavily overflowing its banks.

Lazy summer days and lazy summer rivers. The water is low and slow. The air is warm. Everywhere stand stately redwoods. Pick your activity—biking, hiking, swimming, picnicking, or camping—and select a river site within one of the numerous state parks or Redwood National Park. The swimmers are enjoying the Eel; campers are picnicking along the Smith.

The Rogue River

A River of Three Faces

Its lower face is its most famous face

Emerging from the western slope of the Cascades, the Rogue River winds across farmlands and orchards before making a run through the wilderness. For its last 126 circuitous miles—from Grants Pass to Gold Beach—the Rogue drops 950 feet as it cuts a narrow canyon through the Coast Range. Pines and firs cover the canyon walls at the higher elevations; conifers, oak, maple, and fragrant myrtle blanket the lower slopes. A road parallels the river west as far as Grave Creek and between Illahe and Gold Beach; a 40-mile wilderness trail bridges the roadless gap. But the most popular approach to the Rogue is by boat, either motoring upstream or drifting downstream.

JACK McDOWELL

A variety of wildlife freely roams the Rogue River wilderness. Black-tailed deer **(above)** and Roosevelt Elk browse in side glens and ridges. Otters play in the river. Standing at water's edge are great blue herons fishing for food. Also sighted near the river's bank during salmon runs are black bear, eagerly waiting to snag a catch.

Rogue River Wilderness. For 4 miles, from Grave Creek to Illahe a wilderness trail parallels the enti roadless stretch of the Rogue. If th 5-day hike proves too strenuous, road does enter the trail at Mario In addition to splendid scener vegetation, and wildlife, sigh along the way include an o pioneer cemetery, debris Blossom Bar washed ashore durir the floods of 1964, and Zar Grey's cabin at Winkle Ba

196   Pacific Coastal Basin

Flat-bottomed, high bowed dory-type boats are excellent for drift fishing the Rogue. Similar to the type used on Oregon's McKenzie River, these wooden craft handle the waters of the Rogue well. They drift through the calm current (such as at Alameda Mine **above**) and respond quickly to the oars in rough spots (such as at Tyee Rapids **right**). Floating the Rogue's rapids in rubber rafts is a popular summertime recreation. Float trips, taking anywhere from 3 to 5 days, leave the Grants Pass area. The rapids of the Rogue make canoeing and kayaking unsafe below Grave Creek.

JACK McDOWELL

JACK McDOWELL

The most effortless way to enjoy the Rogue is aboard a power boat on a 64-mile round trip between Gold Beach and Agness. The mail boat **(left)** went into service delivering the mail shortly after the turn of the century. About 20 years later, passengers began to catch a ride. In addition to the mail boat (which still carries the mail), jet boats also make the trip, which includes a two-hour stop for lunch. Jet boats operate seasonally; the mail boat goes year-round.

On Washington's Olympic Peninsula
Sparse rivers amid rain forest runoff

Glacier-created valleys cradle the rivers rising on the western slope of the Olympic Mountains. The area is saturated with rain, but only a few rivers cut across the peninsula. Particularly noteworthy are the Hoh, Queets, and Quinault rivers, each having its own rain forest. An annual average of 150 to 200 inches of rain soak the river valleys where the world's largest specimens of Sitka spruce, Douglas fir, and Western hemlock stand. Of the three "rain forest" river valleys, that of the Hoh is most accessible. An 18-mile hiking trail at the end of the road parallels the river into the forest.

The Soleduck River may not have its own rain forest, but it has a beautiful falls. Surrounded by giant conifers, trailing moss, and lush ferns, Soleduck Falls (also spelled Sol Duc) is reached via a trail from Sol Duc Hot Springs. Although rivers on the western side of the Olympic Mountains can rise rapidly in a downpour, they are remarkably small in volume and number for an area so saturated with rain.

RAY ATKESON

Net gain—about 30 pounds. Natives fish for salmon
with nets from dugout canoes carved out of cedar
logs. For centuries, fishing in the rivers' estuaries and
in the ocean and hunting wild game on shore supported the Indians who made their home on the
western side of the Olympic Peninsula.

The Skagit River
In Washington's Northwest Corner
A river keeping Seattle in light

Colored by dissolving silt from the glaciers of the Cascades, the upper Skagit, largest of the Northern Cascade rivers, cuts through a narrow, 15-mile-long granite gorge. In this gorge lie Gorge, Diablo, and Ross dams, taming the Skagit to provide (along with Boundary Dam on the Pend Oreille River) electricity for the people of the Seattle area. The lakes behind the three dams offer recreation as part of the Ross National Recreation Area. In its lower reaches, the Skagit takes on another personality. Flowing through level terrain, it forms a delta where it empties into Skagit Bay.

Winter resort. *Before emptying into Skagit Bay, a widened Skagit offers a refuge to thousands of great, white snow geese. The Skagit Wildlife Recreation Area on the Pacific Flyway hosts thousands of migratory waterfowl each winter.*

The final approach to Diablo Dam. An incline railway, all that remains of the old Seattle-Skagit River Railway, carries passengers and supplies 600 feet up the steep mountainside in 6 minutes. At the top you can walk to the dam or take a boat ride on Diablo Lake, which affords an excellent view of the waffle-patterned Ross Dam.

A high-altitude experience. *In an alpine setting, slender conifers and snow-capped peaks reflect in Diablo Lake, the middle reservoir in the hydroelectric development on the upper Skagit. Diablo Lake, part of Ross Lake National Recreation Area (which divides North Cascades National Park in two), can be travelled on or alongside of. If you drive the North Cascade Highway, you parallel the path of the Skagit River.*

More Rivers in the Pacific Coastal Basin

Skykomish River. The turbulent Skykomish, making a short and fast descent from the Cascades to the Snoqualmie River near Puget Sound, challenges the skills of kayakers. Paralleled almost entirely by U. S. Highway 2, the Skykomish River in the vicinity of Baring, Washington, takes three falls in 3 miles.

Snoqualmie River. Snow doesn't deter dedicated steelhead fishermen from working the Snoqualmie's icy riffles. Originating in the snowswept western fringes of the Cascade Range, the river runs north to Everett where it empties into Puget Sound. Snoqualmie Falls is a source of hydroelectric power for Seattle.

Green River. Near its origin in the Cascade foothills, the Green cuts more than 200 feet through sedimentary strata, providing a glimpse at millions of years of geologic history. Through the gorge the Green flows blue-green. As the river reaches its demise in Puget Sound between Seattle and Tacoma, its waters become slow and silt-laden.

Siletz River. Born in the Coast Range, the Siletz flows west through pastoral farmlands to its mouth near Kernville on the northern Oregon coast. Picnic sites dot State Highway 229, which follows the twisting river. Around the town of Siletz, spurts of fast water make for exciting innertubing.

CORNELIA FOGLE

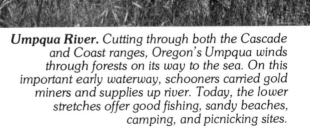

Umpqua River. Cutting through both the Cascade and Coast ranges, Oregon's Umpqua winds through forests on its way to the sea. On this important early waterway, schooners carried gold miners and supplies up river. Today, the lower stretches offer good fishing, sandy beaches, camping, and picnicking sites.

Stillaguamish River. The stillness of the Stillaguamish welcomes early morning fishermen. The river begins as two forks in the Cascade foothills, merges as one near Arlington, and then empties out into a bay.

RAY ATKESON

Pacific Coastal Basin   205

THE GREAT
Where Rivers Never

BASIN
Reach the Sea

Dry Owens Lake, terminus of Owens River

Bounded by the Sierra Nevada on the west and the Wasatch Range on the east, the Great Basin—an almost riverless mass of land—covers 210,000 square miles. The Great Basin takes in a portion of eastern California, almost all of Nevada, a good deal of Utah, and a part of Idaho and Oregon.

What makes the Great Basin different from other western basins? The rivers are land-locked—they are unable to reach the sea. Their terminal points are either lakes or sinks.

Nevada's Humboldt is the Great Basin's most famous river, for it made history as the route of explorers and wagon trains heading for California. Other Great Basin rivers are the Owens in eastern California; the Walker, Carson, and Truckee flowing in eastern California and western Nevada; and the Bear, Jordan, Provo, and Sevier in Utah.

In an area almost equal in size to either the Colorado or the Columbia river basins, there are barely any rivers. The reason is simple. Not enough rain falls in the Great Basin to support major river systems.

Very few settlements dot the Great Basin, for the bulk of the land is desert and water-less. The Truckee River runs through the center of Reno, Nevada; the Jordan and Provo rivers are in the Salt Lake City, Utah, area. A few small towns—the largest is Elko—sit on the Humboldt. Where communities exist on the western side of the basin, river water is conserved for irrigation. Around the eastern Utah area, the rivers are undergoing cleanup programs.

(For a map of the Great Basin and its relation to the rest of the West, turn to either the inside front or back cover.)

THE HUMBOLDT RIVER
Nevada's Big One

A traveler's trail—both past and present—across the Great Basin, the Humboldt runs for 300 miles through the desolate and dry northern Nevada desert

Once a crucial transportation link during the 19th century's westward movement, the Humboldt River today brings life in the form of irrigation and recreation to the flat, dry reaches of northern Nevada. The state's longest river (and the longest river wholly within one state) rises in the mountains of northeastern Nevada. Explorers, gold-seekers, and pioneers picked up its course near its origin and clung to it for more than 300 miles across the sparse Nevada desert until the river disappeared into the Humboldt Sink. Beyond the sink, travelers faced the cruel expanse of the Forty Mile Desert before reaching the Truckee or Carson rivers.

Using the river as a major link in the cross-country route began when Peter Ogden came upon the Humboldt while leading a Hudson's Bay Company expedition for furs. The ill-fated Donner party followed the river west, as did countless other wagon trains. The transcontinental railroad and later Interstate Highway 80 picked up the same route paralleling the river.

Settlements along the Humboldt are few and far between. Towns, such as Winnemucca and Elko, grew up as trading centers, filling the need for way stations on the Humboldt Trail. Today, they are ranching and farming communities as well as traveler stop-over points.

Before 1860, travelers relied on the Humboldt to take them across Nevada into California. But in that year, ranches sprang up along the river, and first attempts were made at using the Humboldt for irrigation. In 1941 the Humboldt Project began operation, and Rye Patch Dam delivered stored river water to fields of alfalfa and wheat.

A Path of History. If the Humboldt could speak, it would have tales to tell, for paralleling the river was the Humboldt Trail, the emigrants' route across the desert. In the 1860s railroad tracks were laid, and in the early 1900s roads were put in—both following the path carved by the pioneers.

Rye Patch Reservoir, sitting amid
dry bluffs, stores the water of the
Humboldt River for irrigation in the
Lovelock Valley. Rye Patch's
smooth surface also accommodates
boaters and fishermen.

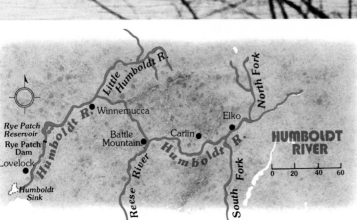

The Humboldt at Work
From Rye Patch—upstream and downstream benefits

Westward-bound emigrants depended on the Humboldt River's trickle of brackish water to keep themselves and their livestock alive. But the relatively few people who chose to settle the parched lands along the Humboldt needed a steady, good, and reliable supply of water. Under the Bureau of Reclamation's Humboldt Project, Rye Patch Dam stores the Humboldt River for irrigation about 26 miles upstream from Lovelock. Principal crops are alfalfa, hay, alfalfa seed, wheat, and barley, grown mostly to feed cattle and sheep that range in the upper Humboldt Basin and in California's Central Valley.

TED STRESHINSKY

TED STRESHINSKY

Rye Patch Dam (above) *is the only control on the Humboldt. Rye Patch Reservoir stores water for irrigation—so crucial for farm productivity in an area receiving an average of 5.76 inches of rain a year. Irrigation season begins around April 15. Water leaves the reservoir, passes through the dam* **(right)**, *and is channeled through the Lovelock Valley to irrigate about 30,000 acres. Gates along the six main canals* **(far right)** *open to allow water to pass to fields.*

TED STRESHINSKY

Two benefits from the Humboldt. *Ranchers around the Elko area rely on the upper Humboldt (fed by snow melt) to irrigate their lands and water their livestock. They also depend on the downstream damming of the river. Water stored behind Rye Patch Dam irrigates fields of feed, grown for the cattle that range in the Humboldt's upper basin.*

Along the Humboldt Trail
Unbelievable sights across an unbelievable land

Most rivers change character between their headwaters and their mouth, but the metamorphosis of the Humboldt is perhaps the most pronounced of all. It is hard to believe that the alkaline trickle of a river disappearing by evaporation and percolation into the barren Humboldt Sink begins as sparkling clear streams in the Ruby, Jarbidge, and Independence mountains. What happens to the Humboldt along its 300-mile trail? Pursuing a desert route and receiving no support from rain, the river disappears into thin air.

TED STRESHINSKY

Carlin Canyon's treacherous terrain was a thorn in the side of emigrants and their wagon trains. With the completion of the transcontinental railway in 1868, travel, not only through the canyon but also across the Nevada desert, was greatly simplified. In 1913 the first road, today's Interstate 80, was routed through Carlin Canyon. Lying between Carlin and Elko, the canyon is probably the Humboldt's most scenic spot.

The end of the trail. By the time the Humboldt reaches the end of its line, it has literally evaporated away. Around Humboldt Sink, vegetation is scarce because of the alkaline soil, lack of water.

A tranquil beginning. Rising in the forested slopes of the Jarbidge, Ruby, and Independence mountains, the Humboldt River's origin is a marked contrast to the desert terrain bordering its path through the thirsty lands of northern Nevada.

Great Basin 213

THE OWENS RIVER
Little Known but Heavily Relied Upon

A lone river along the eastern side of the Sierra, the Owens is diverted halfway along its path from its valley to the people of Los Angeles

The tremendous peaks of the Sierra Nevada rise on the west; the smaller White and Inyo mountains sit to the east. Sunk in the middle is the Owens Valley, a long, deep trough named for the river that passes through it.

The natural headwaters of the Owens River are Big Springs; the terminus is Owens Lake. But the river—diverted below Big Pine through an aqueduct to Los Angeles—never reaches the lake. This leaves the hauntingly beautiful Owens Lake dry, sandy, and pebble-strewn (see pages 206-207), a far cry from the days when steamers hauled ore across the water-filled lake.

The Paiute Indians had the Owens Valley all to themselves until mountain man Joseph Walker arrived in 1834. Soon after, miners, ranchers, and farmers came. Today, a few small communities—Bishop, Lone Pine, Big Pine, Independence—dot the valley.

Lying on the eastern slope of the Sierra, the Owens River is not close to any major metropolitan area. U.S. Highway 395 does parallel the river, which is much closer to Southern California communities than those in Northern California. Although it sits just to the east of Kings Canyon and Sequoia national parks, no roads cross the parks.

The Owens River is not used to any great extent in its own valley. Some fishing occurs in the feeder creeks and in the Big Springs area. Rafts negotiate a small section of river in Bishop, and swimmers soak in Hot Creek. Enough water stays in the valley to irrigate 19,000 acres of land for pasture or alfalfa. But the bulk of the water leaves the valley on a 338-mile journey to Los Angeles to provide that city with its water supply.

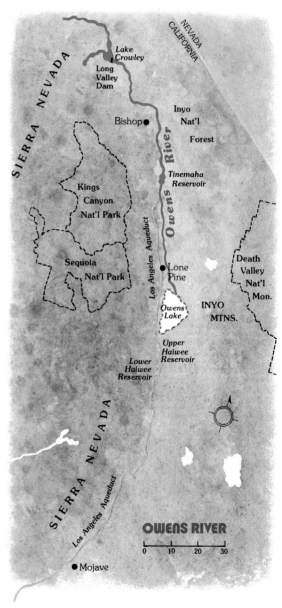

OWENS RIVER

0   10   20   30

Expect the unexpected in the Owens Valley. Although the Owens River is not allowed to be much of a waterway, seasoned anglers know the right trout fishing spots, such as Bishop Creek *(left)*. Roaming the range between Big Pine and Independence are tule elk, the world's smallest and rarest elk. Native Californians, their original home was the Central Valley, but when settlers moved in, the elk population decreased because of hunters or lost grazing grounds. In the 1930s, 27 elk were resettled in the Owens Valley—and it has been considered a successful transplant, with the 1973 population numbering 340.

Great Basin 215

Owen/ River to Lo/ Angele/

The great water caper of 1913

How one feels about what has happened to the Owens River depends on where one lives. To an Owens Valley dweller, it means the loss of a river and a once-green valley. To a resident of Los Angeles, it means one of the reasons that city exists, for the Owens River supplies Los Angeles with the major bulk of its water. In the early 1900s, after several years of drought, city engineers looked to the Owens River as a source of water. They bought land along the river, tributary streams, and the aqueduct route. Then they built the system. The first aqueduct was finished in 1913; an extension was added in 1940. A second aqueduct, paralleling the first, was completed in 1970.

TED STRESHINSKY

A lingering reminder of the past. Nestled at the base of the Sierra Nevada's finely sculptured eastern slope, Round Valley recalls early days in the Owens Valley, when verdant fields rather than arid, scrubby land covered the valley. Presently, about 19,000 acres are irrigated pasture and alfalfa; the remainder is used for dry grazing.

A great engineering feat, the Los Angeles-Owens River Aqueduct carries Owens River water 338 miles from the Owens Valley, over foothills, through mountains, across the Mojave Desert, and into Los Angeles. The original aqueduct, completed in 1913, includes 142 tunnels, 12 miles of inverted steel siphons, 24 miles of unlined conduit, 37 miles of open cement-lined conduit, and 97 miles of covered conduit. In 1940 an 11-mile tunnel was drilled through the Mono Craters to extend the aqueduct north and tap the waters of the Mono Basin. Los Angeles, concerned about the demands on the Colorado River (also a supplier of water to Los Angeles) realized that the amount of water in the Owens River Mono Basin area exceeded what was delivered. To tap this added water supply, the city constructed and completed in 1970 a second aqueduct paralleling the first.

Like an open-air bathtub, Hot Creek is a great place in which to soak.
Fed by numerous hot springs, Hot Creek flows into Lake Crowley,
headwaters of the Owens River.

TED STRESHINSKY

RIVERS THAT GIVE LOS ANGELES ITS WATER

Where does Los Angeles, a city with little rain and no major rivers, obtain water necessary to support approximately 3 million people? Small percentages come from the Los Angeles, Colorado, and Feather rivers, but the major part (80 per cent) comes from the Owens River, which flows through a valley on the eastern slope of the Sierra Nevada.

Los Angeles River. A source of water since a Mexican and Spanish settlement flourished along its banks in 1781, the Los Angeles River appears dry today to the casual observer. But its underground basin, tapped by 105 active wells, provides Los Angeles with about 75 million gallons of water a day.

Colorado and Feather Rivers. As a member of the Metropolitan Water District of Southern California, Los Angeles is entitled to water from the 300-mile-long Colorado River Aqueduct (completed in 1941) and from the California State Water Project (operating in 1973). Los Angeles receives a daily average of 42 million gallons of the Colorado River and is entitled to an annual allotment of 2 million acre feet from the Metropolitan Water District.

Owens River. The majority of water comes from the Owens River. William Mulholland, first superintendent and chief engineer of the city's water department, devised a plan to bring water from the eastern slope of the Sierra, over foothills, through valleys, and across the Mojave Desert to its final destination—the city of Los Angeles. In the early 1900s, two bond issues totaling $24.5 million were approved to purchase land and water rights in the Owens Valley. First water delivery was in 1913 through the 223-mile-long Los Angeles Owens River Aqueduct. Several years later the aqueduct was extended 115 miles to tap four mountain streams in the Mono Basin. This extension involved drilling an 11-mile tunnel through Mono Craters.

With Los Angeles continuously growing and with more water available in the Owens River Mono Basin area than was able to be moved through the original aqueduct, a second aqueduct was completed in 1970 to roughly parallel the original and bring additional water to Los Angeles.

Los Angeles Aqueduct, in the Owens Valley

TED STRESHINSKY

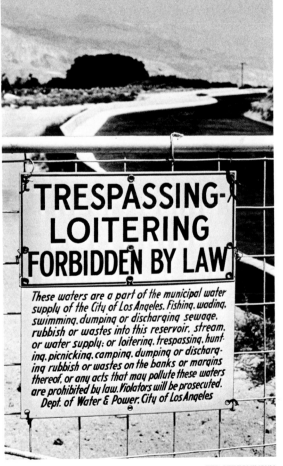

TED STRESHINSKY

Los Angeles Aqueduct, in the Owens Valley

More Rivers in the Great Basin

Truckee River. *Running about 100 miles from Lake Tahoe to Pyramid Lake, the Truckee flows right through the middle of Reno. Several small hydroelectric plants on the river furnish domestic and irrigation water for much of western Nevada. An early day use of the river was for ice—tons were collected from connecting ponds. In the late 1900s, the Truckee served as a highway for logs on their way to the railroad or to lumber mills.*

TED STRESHINSKY

Jordan River. *Flowing 55 miles north through the populated areas between Utah Lake and the Great Salt Lake, the Jordan carries the wastes and debris of Salt Lake City and Provo. The aim of the Jordan River Parkway, a program currently underway, is river clean up and flood control. An additional benefit will be recreational reservoirs.*

PAUL BJORNN

TED STRESHINSKY

Carson River. *Diverted by dams, the Carson irrigates acres of land in the lower Carson Valley near Fallon, Nevada. Lahonton Reservoir stores the natural flow of the Carson as well as water diverted from the Truckee River. Irrigated crops are alfalfa, pasture wheat, barley, small fruits, and vegetables. The Carson River begins on the eastern slopes of the Sierra, then flows across the plains before disappearing in barren Carson Sink.*

Provo River. *A restored railroad takes sightseers across the Provo, up river from dams that supply Salt Lake City and the surrounding communities with water. For a different perspective of the river, you can ride an aerial tram car to the cliffs above Bridal Veil Falls. The Provo's path is from Utah's High Uintas down to Utah Lake.*

CARLA CANNON

BETTY RANDALL

Walker River. *Two forks—the east and the west—merge as one, forming the Walker River. Originating in the eastern slopes of the Sierra, horses pasture in the mountain meadows. Several Walker River Irrigation District reservoirs conserve the Walker's flow. The end of the river is in Walker Lake, a remnant of a sea that once covered much of Nevada.*

Great Basin   221

SUGGESTED READINGS

The following books, pamphlets, and magazine articles deal with specific western rivers and with rivers and river-related topics in general. They should be available at most large libraries and good bookstores or from the publisher. Books and articles that cover only rivers outside the West have not been included in this bibliography.

Books of General Interest

Amos, William H. *The Infinite River.* New York: Random House, 1970.

Bardach, John E. *Downstream: A Natural History of the River.* New York: Harper & Row, 1964.

Braun, Ernest, and Cavagnaro, David. *Living Water.* Palo Alto: American West Publishing Company, 1971.

Brittain, R. E. *Rivers, Man, and Myths.* Garden City, New York: Doubleday and Co., Inc., 1958.

Gresswell, R. Kay, and Huxley, Anthony, eds. *A Standard Encyclopedia of the World's Rivers and Lakes.* New York: G. P. Putnam's Sons, 1965.

Pringle, Laurence. *Wild River.* Philadelphia and New York: J. B. Lippincott Co., 1972.

Sunset Books. *The Beautiful Northwest.* Menlo Park, California: Lane Publishing Co., 1970.

Sunset Books. *The Beautiful Southwest.* Menlo Park, California: Lane Publishing Co., 1972.

Sunset Books. *National Parks of the West.* Menlo Park, California: Lane Publishing Co., 1970.

River of Life. Department of the Interior Environmental Report. Conservation Yearbook Series Vol. 6. Washington, D.C.: U.S. Government Printing Office, 1970.

Usinger, Robert L. *The Life of Rivers and Streams.* New York: McGraw-Hill, Inc., 1967.

Specialized Subjects

Baldwin, Helene L. and McGuinness, C. L. *A Primer on Ground Water.* Department of the Interior Geological Survey. Washington, D.C.: U.S. Government Printing Office, 1963.

Corle, Edwin, *The Gila. River of the Southwest.* New York: Rinehart and Company, Inc., 1951.

Craighead, John and Craighead, Frank. "White-water Adventure on Wild Rivers of Idaho." *National Geographic,* Vol. 137, No. 2, pp. 213–238, February, 1970.

Dana, Julian. *The Sacramento: River of Gold.* New York: Rinehart and Co., 1939.

Feth, J. H. *Water Facts and Figures for Planners and Managers.* Geological Survey Circular 601–1. Washington, D.C.: U.S. Government Printing Office, 1973.

Findley, Rowe. "The Bittersweet Waters of the Lower Colorado." *National Geographic,* Vol. 144, No. 4, pp. 540–569, October, 1973.

Fisher, Anne B. *The Salinas, Up-side Down River.* New York: Farrar & Rinehart, 1945.

Fry, Donald H. Jr. *Anadromous Fishes of California.* Sacramento: State Department of Fish and Game, 1973.

Gulick, Bill. *Snake River Country.* Caldwell, Idaho: The Caxton Printers, Ltd., 1972.

Holbrook, Stewart H. *The Columbia River.* New York: Holt, Rinehart, and Winston, Inc., 1956.

Jenkinson, Michael. *Wild Rivers of North America.* New York: E. P. Dutton and Co., Inc., 1973.

Judge, Joseph. "Retracing John Wesley Powell's Historic Voyage down the Grand Canyon." *National Geographic,* Vol.135, pp. 668–713, May, 1969.

Leopold, Luna B. and Langbein, Walter B. *A Primer on Water.* Department of the Interior Geological Survey. Washington, D.C.: U.S. Government Printing Office, 1970.

Leydet, Francois. *Time and the River Flowing, Grand Canyon.* San Francisco: Sierra Club, 1964.

Lyman, William Denison, *The Columbia River.* Portland: Binfords and Mort, 1963.

Morgan, Dale L. *The Humboldt, Highroad of the West.* New York: Rinehart and Company, 1943.

Morgan, Murray. *The Dam.* Story of Grand Coulee. New York: Barnes & Noble, 1954.

Rivers of California. San Francisco: Pacific Gas and Electric Company, 1962.

"The Salt—Mightiest Little River of them all." *Arizona Highways,* Vol. XLV, No. 9. September, 1969.

Satterfield, Archie. *Moods of the Columbia.* Seattle: Superior Publishing Co., 1968.

Snyder, Gerald S. *In the Footsteps of Lewis and Clark.* Washington, D.C.: National Geographic Society, 1970.

Starbird, Ethel A. "A River Restored: Oregon's Willamette." *National Geographic,* Vol. 141, No. 6, pp. 816–835. June, 1972.

Story of Hoover Dam. Department of Interior. Washington, D.C.: U.S. Government Printing Office, 1971.

The Story of the Columbia Basin Project. Department of the Interior. Washington, D.C.: U.S. Gov't Printing Office, 1964.

Swenson, H. A. and Baldwin, H. L. *A Primer on Water Quality.* Department of the Interior. Washington, D.C.: U.S. Government Printing Office, 1965.

Waters, Frank. *The Colorado.* Rinehart and Company, 1946.

Watkins, T. H. *The Grand Colorado.* Palo Alto: American West Publishing Co., 1969.

Historical Works

DeVoto, Bernard, ed. *The Journals of Lewis and Clark.* Boston: Houghton Mifflin Company, 1953.

Drago, Harry Sinclair. *The Steamboaters.* New York: Bramhall House, 1967.

Mills, Randolph V. *Stern-Wheelers Up Columbia.* Palo Alto: Pacific Books, 1947.

Steamboat Days on the Rivers. Portland: Oregon Historical Society, 1969.

Powell, John Wesley. *Down the Colorado.* Photographs and epilogue by Eliot Porter. New York: E. P. Dutton & Co., Inc., 1969.

Powell, J. W. *The Explorations of the Colorado River and its Canyons.* New York: Dover Publications, Inc., 1961.

Guidebooks

Belknap, Buzz. *Grand Canyon River Guide.* New York, Salt Lake City, San Francisco: Canyonlands Press, 1969.

Harris, Thomas. *Down the Wild Rivers, A Guide to the Streams of California.* San Francisco: Chronicle Books, 1972.

Huser, Verne and Belknap, Buzz. *Snake River Guide.* Boulder City, Nevada: Westwater Books, 1972.

Rivers and Lakes—Explorer's Guide to the West. San Jose: H. M. Gousha Company, 1972.

Sainsbury, George and Hertzog, Nanci. *The Dam Book, Recreation on Washington Reservoirs.* Mercer Island, Washington: Klatawa Enterprises, 1970.

Schumacher, Genny, *Deepest Valley.* A guide to the Owens Valley. Berkeley, California: Wilderness Press, 1969.

INDEX

All-American Canal, 111, 114-117
American River, 11, 12, 174, 176-177, 180
American River Parkway, 170-171
Apache Trail, 148-149

Banks Lake, 36-37
Bear River (California), 176, 180
Bear River (Utah), 207
Bitterroot River, 92
Blue Mesa Dam, 111
Boating, commercial
  Columbia River, 28, 30-31
  the Delta, 172
  Sacramento River, 169
  San Joaquin River, 168
  St. Joe River, 43
  Willamette River, 62-63, 71
Boating, pleasure, 100-101
  (see also rafting)
  Colorado River, 124-126
  Columbia River, 28, 36
  the Delta, 155, 173
  Deschutes River, 79
  Green River, 136
  McKenzie River, 72
  Pend Oreille River, 45
  Rogue River, 152-153, 198-199
  Russian River, 190, 194
  Sacramento River, 164, 168-169
  Salmon River, 98
  Salt River, 144, 149
  San Joaquin River, 164
  Snake River, 96
  Willamette River, 57, 66-67
Bonneville Dam, 17, 20, 22, 24, 25
Boundary Dam, 202
Bridges
  McKenzie River, 73
  Willamette River, 70-71
Bruneau River, 11, 102

Calaveras River, 176, 180
California Aqueduct, 188, 189
California State Water
  Project, 158, 174, 188-189
Carson River, 207, 221
Cataract Canyon, 130-131
Celilo Falls, 9, 16
Central Arizona Project, 12, 111
Central Valley Project, 10, 154, 158, 162-165, 174
Chief Joseph Dam, 20
Clark Fork, 40, 45
Clearwater River, 11, 103
Coachella Canal, 111, 114
Coastal Rivers, 190-203
Coeur d'Alene River, 11, 15, 40, 42
Colorado River, 9, 10, 12, 92, 105, 106-110, 111, 112-127, 157, 193, 219
Colo. River Aqueduct, 111, 219
Colo. River Basin, 8, 9, 104-151
Colorado River Storage
  Project, 111, 128, 151
Columbia Basin Project, 10, 36-39
Columbia Gorge, 34-35
Columbia River, 9, 12, 14-15, 16-39, 92, 157, 193
Columbia River Basin, 8, 9, 14-103
Coolidge Dam, 151
Coquille River, 190
Coulees, 36-37
Cove Palisades State Park, 74, 76, 79
Crooked River, 74, 75, 76-77, 81

The Dalles Dam, 9, 20
Damming, 7, 9-10
Davis Dam, 111
The Delta, 154, 155, 172-173
Deschutes River, 11, 15, 74-81, 92
Diablo Dam, 202
Dolores River, 11, 150
Dories, 72, 101, 198
Dry Falls, 37
Dworshak Dam, 103

Eel River, 11, 12, 92, 180, 190, 192, 193, 195

Feather River, 92, 174, 176, 180, 183, 184-185, 188-189, 193, 219
Ferry boats
  Columbia River, 16, 28-29
  Willamette River, 57
Fish counting stations, 24
Fish ladders, 25
Fishing, commercial
  Columbia River, 26
Fishing, sport
  Clark Fork, 45
  Columbia River, 26
  the Delta, 155
  Deschutes River, 79
  Green River, 137
  Klamath River, 192
  McKenzie River, 72
  Merced River, 179
  Middle Fork of the Feather, 185
  Owens River, 215
  Quinault River, 201
  Salt River, 149
  Snoqualmie River, 204
  Stanislaus River, 175, 186
  Stillaguamish River, 205
  Willamette River, 68-69
  Yakima River, 48
Flaming Gorge Dam, 111, 128
Flathead River, 11
Floods, 193
Folsom Dam, 174
Fontenelle Dam, 128
Franklin D. Roosevelt Lake, 28, 29, 36, 37
Friant Dam, 162, 163

Geology
  Colorado River, 109, 123
  Columbia River, 34, 36-37
  Crooked River, 76-77
  Deschutes River, 74, 76, 79
  Green River, 128
  Green River (Washington), 204
  John Day River, 74, 76
  Metolius River, 76
  Gila River, 11, 92, 105, 111, 140-141, 151
  Glen Canyon Dam, 106, 110, 111, 125
  Gorge Dam, 202
  Grand Canyon, 106, 109, 118-123
  Grand Coulee Dam, 20, 36, 37, 38
  Grande Ronde River, 96
  Great Basin, 8, 206-221
  Green River, 11, 105, 111, 128-133, 136-137
  Green River (Washington), 190, 204
  Gunnison River, 11, 105, 111, 151

Hells Canyon, 96-97
Hells Canyon Dam, 96
Hetch Hetchy Reservoir, 174, 182
Hoh River, 83, 153, 190, 200
Hoover Dam, 10, 106, 110, 111, 112-113, 126, 193
Humboldt River, 92, 207, 208-213
Hydroelectric power, 23

Idaho Power Company, 93
Illinois River, 11
Imperial Dam, 111, 114
Irrigation
  Carson River, 221
  Colorado River, 111, 114-117
  Columbia Basin Project, 10, 36-39
  the Delta, 172
  Humboldt River, 209, 210-211
  Kern River, 161
  Kings River, 181
  Sacramento River, 154, 158-161
  Salt River, 147
  San Joaquin River, 154, 158-161
  Snake River, 91, 93
  Wenatchee River, 48, 49, 50, 51
  Yakima River, 48, 49, 50, 51

John Day Dam, 20
John Day River, 11, 15, 74-81, 92
Jordan River, 10, 207, 220

Kern River, 161, 180
Kings River, 10, 174, 178, 180, 181
Klamath River, 11, 153, 190, 192, 193
Kootenai River, 15, 102

Lake Chinook, 76, 78, 79
Lake Havasu, 106, 111, 124
Lake Mead, 106, 110, 111, 124-125
Lake Mojave, 106, 124
Lake Oroville, 174
Lake Powell, 106, 111, 125
Lewis and Clark, 16, 18-19, 98, 103
Lewis and Clark River, 32
Little Colo. River, 104-105, 121
Locks, 17, 30-31
Los Angeles Owens River
  Aqueduct, 216-217, 219
Los Angeles River, 219

Mad River, 190, 192
Mattole River, 190, 192
McKenzie River, 8-9, 72-73
McNary Dam, 20
Merced River, 92, 174, 176, 178-179, 180
Metolius River, 74, 76, 82-83
Metropolitan Water District
  of Southern Calif., 111, 113
Middle Fork of the Feather, 11, 174, 182-185
Middle Fork of the Salmon, 11, 15, 98, 99
Minam River, 11
Mokelumne River, 174, 176, 180
Morelos Dam, 117
Morrow Point Dam, 111
Moyie River, 11

Navajo Dam, 111
Nehalem River, 190

Okanogan River, 103
Oroville Dam, 174, 188, 193
Owens River, 83, 92, 206-207, 214-218, 219
Owyhee River, 11, 103

Pacific Coastal Basin, 8, 152-205
Pacific Gas and Electric
  Company, 174, 180, 194
Paddle wheelers, 157
Palouse River, 102
Parker Dam, 111
Pelton Dam, 79
Pend Oreille River, 15, 40-47, 92, 202
Pit River, 180
Port of Portland, 28, 33, 56, 62-63
Port of Sacramento, 168-169
Port of Stockton, 168
Powell, John Wesley, 108-109, 128
Priest Rapids Dam, 20
Priest River, 11, 40, 42, 45
Provo River, 207, 221

Queets River, 153, 190, 200
Quinault River, 153, 190, 200-201

Rafting, 11, 12, 100, 134-135
  American River, 171
  Colorado River, 106, 118-123
  Deschutes River, 79
  Green River, 130-133
  Owyhee River, 103
  Salmon River, 98-99
  Smith River, 194
  Snake River, 86-87
  Spokane River, 44
  Stanislaus River, 186
  Tuolumne River, 186-187
  Willamette River, 67
  Yampa River, 151

Rock Island Dam, 20
Rocky Reach Dam, 20-21
Rogue River, 11, 152-153, 190, 196-199
Roosevelt Dam, 144, 145
Ross Dam, 202
Round Butte Dam, 74, 78, 79
Russian River, 190, 192, 193, 194
Rye Patch Dam, 208, 209, 210

Sacramento River, 9, 92, 153, 154-169, 180, 193
Salmon
  counting stations, 24
  effect of damming, 24
  fish ladders, 25
  life cycle, 27
  migratory habits, 24, 27
Salmon fishing
  Columbia River, 9, 26
  Deschutes River, 78
  Klamath River, 192
  Quinault River, 201
  Willamette River, 68-69
Salmon River, 11, 98-99
Salt River, 92, 111, 138-149
Salt River Canyon, 142-143
Salt River Project, 10, 138, 144-147
San Joaquin River, 92, 153, 154-169, 180, 181
San Juan River, 105, 111, 150
Sevier River, 207
Shasta Dam, 154, 162, 163, 193
Shoshone Falls, 84
Sierra Rivers, 174-179, 180, 181-189
Siletz River, 190, 205
Siuslaw River, 190
Skagit River, 153, 190, 202-203
Skykomish River, 190, 204
Smith River, 11, 92, 153, 190, 191, 192, 194, 195
Smith Rock, 76-77, 81
Snake River, 15, 84-91, 92, 93-97, 166, 193
Snake River Canyon, 95
Snake River Plain, 90-91, 93-95
Snoqualmie River, 190, 204
Soleduck River, 190, 200
Spokane River, 9, 10, 11, 15, 40-47
Stanislaus River, 12, 174, 175, 176, 180, 186
St. Joe River, 11, 15, 32, 40, 42-43, 166
Stillaguamish River, 190, 205
Sunnyside Dam, 48

Trinity Lake, 164
Trinity River, 180
Truckee River, 92, 207, 220
Tule River, 180
Tumwater Canyon, 48, 54-55
Tuolumne River, 92, 174, 176, 180, 182, 186-187

Umpqua River, 190, 205
Upriver Dam, 40-41

Walker River, 207, 221
Wanapum Dam, 20
Wells Dam, 20
Wenatchee River, 15, 48-55
Wild and Scenic Rivers Act, 11, 98, 103, 182, 190
Wildlife, 166-167
  Colorado River, 122, 123
  Rogue River, 196
  Sacramento River, 165
  Salmon River, 98-99
  San Joaquin River, 165
  Snake River, 87, 88-89, 95
  Willamette River, 9, 10, 14-15, 56-71, 92

Yakima River, 15, 48-55
Yampa River, 151
Yaquina River, 190
Yuba River, 180

This book was printed and bound by Kingsport Press, Kingsport, Tennessee, from litho film prepared by Balzer-Shopes Litho Plate Company, San Francisco, California. Body type is Souvenir, type for heads is Blippo Black, composed by Holmes Typography Inc., San Jose, California. Paper for pages is Sterling Enamel made by Westvaco, Luke, Maryland.

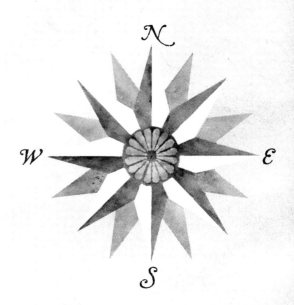

Western Rivers and their Watersheds

The Continental Divide—a massive mountain range running north and south through the western part of the North American continent—has determined the course of much United States history and many of its rivers. Although Lewis and Clark crossed the divide in the early 1800s charting an inland water route to the Pacific Ocean, it would be another half century before explorers and scouts really opened up the interior of this country for westward expansion.

Just as it has governed the flow of people, the Great Divide exerts a profound effect on the pattern of North American rivers. At its top is the point that determines the direction rivers will flow. Water hitting the eastern slope of the divide heads for the Atlantic Ocean; water born on the western side journeys to the Pacific Ocean. On the western side of the divide, rivers fall into four groupings: the Columbia River Basin, the Colorado River Basin, the Pacific Coastal Basin, and the Great Basin.